ANNIHILATE ME VOLUME 2

A NOVEL BY

CHRISTINA ROSS

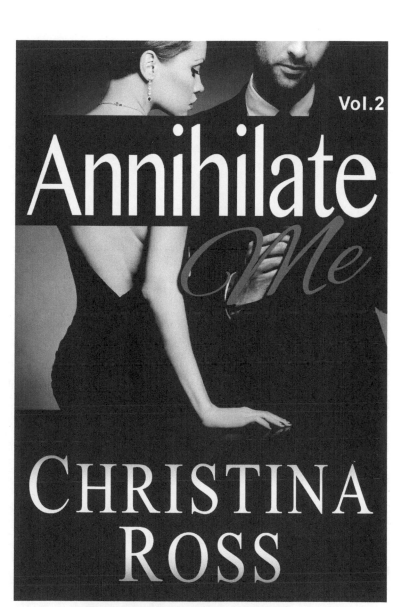

Vol.2

Annihilate
Me

CHRISTINA
ROSS

For my parents.

And for strong-willed women everywhere.

This book begins with the two final chapters of *Annihilate Me, Vol. 1*, to remind readers of where we left off...for key reasons.

Enjoy!

ANNIHILATE ME
VOLUME 2

BY

CHRISTINA ROSS

BOOK ONE

CHAPTER ONE

New York City
September

When the elevator doors opened, Alex stood beyond them, just as he had the last time, with his hands in his pockets and a grin on his face.

Only this time wasn't like the last time. This time was different. We were moving in a new direction that became immediately apparent when he held out his hand for mine and drew me close to him. He kissed me lightly on the lips. Then, in my ear, in a voice that was so low, it was beyond sexy, he said, "You look beautiful."

"Thank you."

He admired my dress. "That should get some attention."

"It might even blind a few people."

He arched an eyebrow at me. "It would make for an interesting night if it did." He reached out and gently touched my hair. "I love it when you wear your hair down."

"I know you do."

"Did you do it for me?"

"I might have given it a thought."

"I'm glad that you did. Do you remember when we officially met? At the interview? We were talking, you pulled out a pin in your hair, it tumbled down your back, and I was transfixed. Then, it was wavy. Now, it's straight. Either way, I love it. When I think of you, this is how I imagine you. With your hair down. With it falling down your back. With you shaking it out with your hands in an effort to cool yourself, if only for an instant."

I could feel myself starting to get warm. "Here," I said, wanting to take the attention off me. "Let me have a look at you." I pulled away from him, and he put his hands back in his pockets, cocked his head to one side, and grinned. "Very handsome, Mr. Wenn."

"Thank you, Ms. Kent."

"But then I love you in a tux. *And* in a suit."

"Why's that?"

"If we were to psychoanalyze the situation, it likely would come down to some Prince Charming fantasies I had as a kid. You know, someone who would sweep me away from all that I wanted to forget."

"What did you want to forget?"

"I've forgotten," I lied. "And it doesn't matter now, because here he is. Right in front of me."

"You don't say?"

"I do say."

"Why do I want to devour you right now?"

"Probably for the same reasons I want to tackle you. But Bernie worked hard, so we'll respect that."

"We better change the subject or my hands are going to be all over you."

"And that's a bad thing?"

"Jennifer...."

"Blackwell and I had fun today," I said. "I don't know how she does it, but that woman is nothing if not on her game."

"She always has been. My mother loved her for it. I've always thought they should name a hurricane after her."

"It would need to be Category 5. Why shortchange her?"

"Good point." He paused for a moment. "Would you mind turning around for me? Just so I can see the rest of the dress?"

I started to turn, but then he put his hand on my shoulder and stopped me so my back was to him. "I want to have a long look," he said. "Do you mind?"

His hand resting on my bare shoulder was almost enough to do me in. But then he removed it and I heard him take a step back.

"Did you pick this out?"

"Blackwell did."

"Blackwell has an eye." His voice was off to my left. Then, I heard him come up behind me. "In fact, I know she does. With her help, I picked out this."

Over my head came a diamond and sapphire necklace that made me catch my breath when I caught a glimpse of it as he moved my hair aside and fastened it around me. *Blackwell*, I thought. *Missing a necklace, indeed.*

The stones were cool against my neck. "Alex," I said.

"My gift to you."

"But all of this is a gift from you."

"May I see?"

I turned to him with my hand pressed against the stones.

"You'll need to lower your hand, Jennifer."

"Sorry. I don't know what to say."

"I say it's beautiful. What do you think? There's a mirror to your left. Look."

I turned and saw that the necklace was in the same family as the other jewels. A delicate clutch of diamonds circled my neck, followed by a single, vertical line of three larger diamonds at my throat. At the end of that was a large teardrop sapphire surrounded by smaller diamonds that set just above my cleavage.

"It's gorgeous," I said. "I don't know what to say."

"There's no need to say anything."

"Yes, there is." I kissed him, but not as gently as before. I pressed against him with every bit of raw emotion I had within me. I leaned full into his kiss, which probed deep. With his body so close to mine, I could feel all of him against me, some of it pulsing. When we pulled away, the collateral damage was clear—he was practically wearing my lipstick. "Here," I said, opening the clutch Blackwell let me borrow. "Tissues. Let me fix that."

"Before you do, how about this first?" He went in for the kill again. Only this time, his hands smoothed down my sides and rested on my ass, which he squeezed, and then gripped. He pulled me firmly against him so I knew exactly what he was feeling.

My nipples hardened when he did that. A shiver shot through me. I'd never experienced anything like this before, but then I'd never dated anyone before. Still, plenty of other men had tried to catch my eye over the years. Why was this so different? Why did I feel such a strong connection to Alex? Is this what it felt like when you met the 'one'? I had no idea. I wished Lisa were here so I could ask her, because she'd know. She'd been in two long-term relationships. She'd be able to tell me what I was feeling, and why. As for me, this was foreign territory. He'd turned me on so much that I was dizzy with desire. When he kissed me, it felt as if my heart was shaking. A moment later, when he stopped with a gentle bite to my lower lip that obviously was designed to send me to the outer reaches of the universe, where I thought I saw a comet or a nebula, I somehow managed to pull it together and look at him.

"You're going to do me in."

"That's the plan."

"I'm glad you have a plan. Very resourceful of you. And by the way, what was that?"

"What was what?"

"That bite thing you did?"

"Just something I thought you might like. Was I wrong?"

"You weren't wrong."

"You should see what else I can do with my teeth and my tongue."

"Stop."

"No, really. You should see."

"Alex."

"Why are your eyes unfocused?"

"Because I can't handle being manhandled." I lifted my head to the ceiling and collected myself. When I looked at him again, I saw the mischief in his eyes. "Why are you doing this to me?"

"Because you want me to."

I didn't know how to respond to that, so I said, "I need to blot your lips again."

"Please do."

I blotted.

"Am I good to go?" he asked.

"One more swipe."

"I kind of like you on my lips."

"I kind of like *me* on your lips."

"You might want to look in the mirror," he said.

"Oh, no." I looked and saw that my lipstick was gone, but at least it hadn't smeared. After all of Bernie's work, that would have been a disaster. I pulled out the tube of lipstick Blackwell left for me in the clutch and reapplied.

"Are we finished?" I asked.

"For now."

"Then let's get out of here before we decide to stay."

* * *

When we arrived at the museum, the building's facade was lit in bright oranges and deep reds. People were walking up the wide stone steps to the entrance.

Camera flashes popped. The steps were roped off to allow entrance only for the guests, but there were crowds on the sidelines and they were cheering. I remembered what Blackwell said—this was a major draw for celebrities. Given the sheer amount of photographs that were being taken, that appeared to be an understatement.

"Are you nervous?" Alex asked.

"Not at all."

"Get ready for the press."

"They need to get ready for my dress. I'm about to be lit up like a disco ball."

"Who better?" he asked.

* * *

We were twenty minutes inside the Theodore Roosevelt Rotunda—the walls of which also were set ablaze with concealed orange lighting—when I saw a man looking directly at Alex and me.

Given the distraction of the towering and show-stopping brontosaurus skeleton, the crowds—and the famous faces within the crowds—I was surprised that I noticed him at all. But he was looking so openly at us, and with such anger, it was difficult to miss him. He was an older man, somewhere in his late fifties, and he looked familiar to me. I'd seen him before.

Where?

I lifted my martini to my lips and spoke, but didn't sip. "Why is that man staring at us?"

"Which man?"

"Near the skeleton. Gray hair. Fifties. Very tan. He's looked away a few times, but he keeps turning back. He's looking at us now, and he looks pissed. Who is he?"

"Someone who would rather see me dead."

I looked up at him. "That's kind of harsh."

"It's the truth."

"What are you talking about?"

"Let's walk over here."

We joined the milling crowds and stopped beside one of the glowing walls, which Alex leaned against, thus keeping his back to the mystery man and me squarely facing him so we could talk in private.

"His name is Gordon Kobus."

"Kobus Airlines," I said. "Of course. I knew I knew him. His company is about to go under. I've read about it."

Alex shook his head at me. "Jennifer, what don't you know?"

"I told you I'm a business junkie. I live for this stuff. Just don't ever ask me to sew anything for you. Like a button on one of your suits. I'd ruin it, and that would kill me for reasons you already know."

"Noted."

"Kobus just applied for emergency funding from the government."

"It did."

"One of the stories said that the board is also seeking new investors. But they likely won't have time to secure either. Because of the size and the good condition of the fleet, too many are ready to sweep in and take over the company for themselves, hostile or otherwise." And then I just looked at Alex when it came to me. "Which is you, right? Wenn Air. You're planning a takeover. You want to add his fleet to your own."

It wasn't a question it was a statement.

"I do," Alex said. "We're in the early stages now—we're wooing management in an effort to get them on our side, which hasn't exactly been difficult. They're finished with him. He knows it, and you're right—Gordon isn't having any of it." He shrugged. "I don't blame him. Kobus used to be his baby, but he's put baby in the corner for years. He didn't mind the store. He's lived a playboy lifestyle for a decade now, he didn't listen to his board, he didn't listen to counsel, and now it's all caught up with him. I plan on taking his company from him and merging it with my own. We'll give his fleet Wenn's first-class treatment, and manage it successfully."

"How soon?"

He shrugged. "Not sure. Depends on management. But these things take time. If they're for it, we can finish this by winter. If they resist, then we get more aggressive. We apply pressure, and then we make our intentions public. Then it really gets ugly. Either way, we're going forward with it."

I clinked my martini glass against his and we knocked them back.

"That was refreshing," I said.

"The martini or the talk of the takeover?"

"Both."

He looked at me sincerely. "I'm glad you're here, Jennifer. I don't think you know what it means to me. I could talk with you all night. I know it's still early, but I hope you're having a good time."

I certainly was back at Wenn. "I just talked about takeovers with someone who not only understands what they are, but who actually does them. Are you joking? I'm in my element. Oh, and by the way, I look like I'm straight out of *Gatsby* and I have the night's smartest, best-looking date. Because of you, I'm having a fabulous time."

I took his free hand in mine and our fingers interlocked. There were no other words to express how I felt. He tightened his grip, and then he leaned forward to give me a quick peck on the cheek.

"Your stubble is going to do me in."

"You like that?"

"Please, don't tease me."

"You haven't even seen me tease you yet," he said.

* * *

Later, when dinner was announced, we followed the crowd to Milstein Hall, which caused me to pause when we descended the steps that led to the massive space. It was lit in rippling hues of blue that evoked the ocean, and it was filled with fifty tables set for ten. Hovering just below the glass ceiling was an enormous replica of a blue whale that I thought had to be close to a hundred feet long. I'd never seen anything like it. It was magical.

My father entered my head again and started his bullshit rant about how I didn't belong here, but I mentally shook him away. Or at least, I tried to. I looked around at the sea of celebrities, people I had seen for years on television and in movies, or musicians I admired, and I knew he was right. Who was I to be here? It made no logical sense.

But I am here, I thought. And *I'm here for a reason. Where did these people come from? Did all of them come from a privileged life? Or did they work for it? I'm betting most worked for it. I bet, just like me, most never thought they'd see anything like this.*

"Are you OK?" Alex asked.

I realized I was gripping his hand more firmly than before, and I forced myself to relax. "I'm fine. It's just so much. It's beautiful."

At the bottom of the stairs, one of the hosts greeted us and took us to our table, where none other than Immaculata Almendarez herself was seated.

"This should be interesting," I said quietly.

"She planned it," he said. "So, it *will* be interesting. Get ready."

Naturally, when the host seated us, Alex was placed directly beside Immaculata, while I was asked to take the seat between him and an older gentleman.

"Alex," Immaculata said, turning to look at him. "What a surprise."

"Really? I was thinking, 'What a coincidence.'"

"You're so funny." She leaned forward to look at me, and I saw her eyes go to the diamonds and sapphires at my ears, neck and wrist. "And I see you're still with Jane."

"It's Jennifer," I said.

"Right, right. Why do I always think of you as a Jane?"

"I'm not sure, Immaculata. The only thing I can imagine is that as we get older, our capacity to remember things begins to fail."

"It begins to what?"

"Fail. Like our hearing, for instance. You should have yours checked. Our bodies eventually betray us."

"Mine hasn't yet," she said as she pressed her fingertips against the table, and arched her back toward them and it, thus allowing us all to glimpse the full weight of her formidable breasts, which were barely covered by her plunging black dress. I thought she looked desperate, and I didn't mind when she reached for Alex's hand when she turned her attention to him. "How are you?" she asked.

"Working hard, Immaculata."

"You always work so hard."

"Not as much since I've been with Jennifer, but work is work. And work is good." He casually removed his hand from hers and signaled for a waiter. "Wenn keeps me busy. Jennifer keeps me busy in other ways."

Immaculata swallowed that poison pill as if it was a clear glass of water. I had to give it to her—she was cool. "The last time I saw you was two weeks ago. At The Met fundraiser. I saw you both leave in such a hurry. Everyone was buzzing about it."

Oh, she wasn't going to go there.

"There was an undercurrent," she said. "It didn't look good. People said Jennifer removed her jewels and then some overheard a choice exchange of words. It was on everyone's lips for a week. I've been worried about you, especially because I haven't seen you."

She was talking to him as if I wasn't at the table. I rested my chin in the palm of my hand, turned to her, and just listened with a half-smile.

The waiter Alex signaled stopped by the table.

"Would you like a drink, sir?"

"Actually, we'd like another table. I see only half the room is seated at this point, so it shouldn't be an issue. Please tell your host that Alexander Wenn and Jennifer Kent would prefer to be seated elsewhere. Or I can do that for you."

"I'd be happy to assist you, sir."

Conversation at the table stopped. Everyone who was pretending not to listen to Immaculata's conversation with Alex started to listen and watch openly as the moment stretched and unfolded.

"Alex," Immaculata said. "I didn't mean—"

"Yes, you did. You meant everything. And I'm tired of it. I don't play games—ever. You will not insult Jennifer—ever—even if you fail when you try to do so. She's smarter and quicker than you. You should have learned that by now."

"I don't know what you're talking about."

One man at the opposite end of the table cleared his throat.

I felt a sudden rush of affection for Alex. He was finished with her. He pushed back his chair and stood, and then he gently pulled back my chair so I could stand next to him.

"Have a fine evening, Immaculata," Alex said. "And please remember what you learned in boarding school."

"Boarding school?"

"That's right, boarding school."

"What did I learn in boarding school?"

"Obviously not your manners, because they have been absent since we were seated next to you. Good night."

He took my hand and turned to find the host. "Is there another table for us? Or should we leave?"

"Of course there's another table for you, Mr. Wenn. Right this way."

"Thank you," he said.

As we cut through the crowd, he pulled me near him in such a way that was at once protective, possessive, and apologetic. "I'm not going to promise that won't happen again, but if it does with another person, the results will be the same. No one treats you like that in front of me."

He was furious. I could feel his anger coming off him in waves.

"It's OK," I said, wanting to calm him down. "I got in a few licks."

"You did," he said. "But this town can go to hell before that happens again. And I'm sorry that it happened. We never should have sat next to her in the first place. I should have known better. I should have asked for another table when I saw that she'd set us up. I wasn't thinking. I apologize."

I dodged a waiter coming toward us with a lifted tray of cocktails, ducked my head, heard his apology, and kept moving. "There's no need to."

"Yes, there is."

"Then, thank you."

"You're my girlfriend," he said. "There's no need to thank me. No one treats my girlfriend like that. OK?" He turned to look at me, and I could see on his face just how furious he was with the situation. "OK?"

"OK," I said.

He put his hand against my back, and we walked together toward our new table. He'd just called me his girlfriend twice, and this was only our second legitimate date. That is, if we were considering burgers at the diner a date. What the hell was I to make of that?

Nothing.

Because, if I was being honest with myself, what he just said is exactly what I wanted to hear, though I'd never admit it to him. Not yet. We'd moved beyond the past and into another stage. To him, I was his girlfriend. And I was as thrilled about it as I was nervous about it.

What the hell was I going to do when he wanted to become intimate?

CHAPTER TWO

The next week passed in a blur. And while I didn't see Alex as much as I wanted to because we both worked nights—me at the restaurant, he at the events he needed to attend—we met twice for breakfast, we spoke when we could by phone, we texted each other throughout the day, and he always picked me up when the restaurant closed.

Each night, he was fresh from a party and in a tuxedo, looking dashing. Though increasingly, he also looked either distracted or stressed. Tonight was no exception.

When I left the restaurant, he was leaning against the limousine with his feet crossed at the ankles and his arms folded across his chest. He smiled when he saw me, and we kissed for a long, lingering moment, but something was off. I could sense it, and I had to wonder if he was having second thoughts about reigniting this relationship, probably because we still hadn't slept together. By today's standards, that should have happened after the event at the museum. But, despite his efforts, it didn't.

At the end of the night, he asked me up to his penthouse at Wenn and made an effort to progress in that direction, but I told him I wasn't ready. He said there was no hurry, but he might go nuts if he had to wait much longer. He had no clue that I was still a virgin. And he didn't know the reasons why I was still a virgin. At some point, if I was going to continue this relationship with him, I would have to tell him all that I needed to tell him about me and my past. Sooner rather than later. It was unfair to him otherwise.

When we were in the limousine, I put my hand on his leg, and he wrapped his arm around my shoulder. "Hey," he said.

"How do you feel about taking me to your place tonight?" I asked. "I need to talk to you about something. Well, a few things, actually."

"Is everything all right?"

"I just need to talk to you, Alex."

"That sounds ominous."

He lived on the top two floors of Wenn, where his parents once lived. The space was now his. When I first saw it, I wasn't surprised to find how beautifully designed and decorated it was. Save for the colorful, original paintings on the walls, everything was white, from the furniture to the marble floors. At this height, the city views beyond the sweeping surround of windows were spectacular.

"Would you like something to drink?" he asked when we stepped out of his private elevator and into the foyer.

"A martini would be nice."

"You *are* a martini girl, aren't you?"

"Guilty."

"Actually, after today, I wouldn't mind one myself. Give me a few minutes. If you'd like, take off your shoes and relax in the living room. You've been on your feet all night."

"You sound tense," I said as I moved into the room.

"A little. But we'll save talking about that for another time. Right now, I just want to be with you."

Why is he tense?

I looked out at the views, listened to him shake our drinks in the kitchen, and then turned to him when he entered the living room with them. He handed me mine, and we touched glasses. He kissed me meaningfully on the mouth, and we took a sip before sitting down next to each other on the leather sofa.

"Have I told you that you look beautiful tonight, Jennifer?"

"Maybe once or twice. And I'll repeat—you look very handsome yourself, Mr. Wenn."

"How was work?"

"Busier than usual. You?"

We sat on the sofa.

"Another time. What's on your mind? You've made me curious."

My stomach started to turn, but there was no stopping this now. I had to go through with it. I took a sip of my martini, and put it on the table in front of us. "Alex, I need to tell you something."

He didn't respond. He just stared at me, concern and maybe even a trace of fear on his face. But why fear? Did he think I was going to break this off?

"This is going to sound ridiculous," I said. "I'm twenty-five, for God's sake."

"Jennifer, nothing you have to say to me is going to sound ridiculous."

"Are you sure? Because here's one for you. I've never been with anyone before."

His brow furrowed as if he didn't understand.

Just say it.

"I'm a virgin."

His eyes widened. "You're a virgin?"

I nodded and felt a rush of shame. There were reasons why I had never given myself to a man. Reasons that made me feel insecure in this relationship now.

"Is that why, you know, the other night...?"

"That's right."

A weight seemed to lift off him. And there was something else, something in his eyes. A thrill? He reached for my hand. "You didn't need to tell me that."

"Yes, I did. You needed to know. I can't expect you to wait for me forever. And I didn't want to send you mixed signals, or make you feel that I didn't want to be with you, because I do. I want to be with you more than anything. I think about it all the time. But there's something bigger behind this. It's one of the reasons I blew up at you at The Met fundraiser. It's the reason why I protect myself so fiercely. It's something from my past that sometimes creeps into the present."

"You don't have to talk about this."

"Yes, I do."

"Not if you feel unsafe."

"I do feel safe. I need to get this out into the open and just be done with it. When I tell you, you might be finished with me. You might think, 'too much baggage.'"

"I seriously doubt that."

"OK. Well, when I was a kid, my father beat me. He'd get drunk, and he'd take out his anger on me and my mother, who never reported him to the authorities or to child services. I'm not going to go through the laundry list of all that he did to us, but you need to understand that sometimes those memories come flooding back. I have trust issues with men because of it. I still have nightmares about what he did to me, which is another reason I didn't stay the other night. I didn't want to freak you out if I had one."

He studied me for a moment. "I reminded you of your father that night at the Four Seasons, didn't I? You saw something in me that frightened you. That's why you stayed away. I made you think of your father, didn't I?"

"To a degree, yes."

"Jennifer, I'm sorry."

"Alex, this isn't meant to be a guilt trip. It's just so you have a deeper understanding of who I am. I'm twenty-five, and I have zero experience with men beyond my father's abuse. I know you can sense me holding back. I needed you to know that it's not you. It's me."

"No, it isn't." He put his drink beside mine and moved closer to me. "It's him. I'm not going to ask what he did to you. That will come in time, or it won't come at all. It's your choice. The only question I have is whether it was sexual. Because if it was, and if you need additional time to feel like you can trust me before being intimate with me, that's not an issue. When and if it happens, it will just make that moment better."

"None of it was sexual. He just abused me verbally and physically."

"Just?"

"Just. It could have been worse. A lot worse. And to be honest with you, I don't know if I want to wait much longer. Everything in my life is positive right now. I'm in a good space. I'm with a good man. I know you're a good man. I know that night at the Four Seasons was a blip. I get it now. And I'm tired of having my father hold me back. He's not going to do so forever. It's time to get on with it."

"It's time to get on with what?"

I just looked at him. My emotions raw and naked. I felt fully exposed and vulnerable at that moment, but also safe with him.

He was looking hard at me. "What's the other reason you wanted to come here tonight, Jennifer?"

"I didn't have a reason until a moment ago."

"What is it?"

It was difficult for me to say the words, but I forced myself to. "I want to be with you. I feel like I've cheated myself by waiting so long. I've lost years because of my hangups. And now here you are, the one man I can see myself with. I think that when we begin, I'm not going to want to stop. Even now it's difficult for me not to touch you. And I want to touch you."

A darkness that was brooding with desire came over his face. His eyes, framed by his thick lashes, narrowed slightly. "Where do you want to touch me?"

"Everywhere," I said.

"You've thought a lot about this, haven't you?"

More than you know. I nodded and felt myself begin to tremble.

"What was the last thought you had?" There was a roughness to his voice that had never been there before. It was intoxicating.

"Touching your chest. Finally seeing it."

"When was this?"

"At work tonight."

"What brought that on?"

I started to feel hot. "*You* did. I thought of you, and then my mind went there. I want to know every inch of your body. I want to know it better than you do."

He wasn't touching me. He wasn't judging me. He was just listening to me and watching me, but in a way that was different. It was as if he was planning what he was going to do to me. There was a predatory look in his eyes.

"Jennifer, how far do you want to take this?"

"All the way."

"That can be pretty far, and you don't even know how far I'll go. I need to warn you of that, because I will go far. And once I start, it will be a long time before I stop."

"I don't care so long as I feel safe. But I want it to build. I want to be surprised. I want to learn and I don't want you to hold back. If there's something you like to do or that you're into, I want to try it. I want to experience everything."

"Everything?"

"I want you to teach me what you know."

"Are you sure about that?"

"I am."

"That could take some time, you know? And stamina."

"I've got both."

"I can take you to places by barely touching you that will send you out of your body."

"Then do it," I said. "Do it now."

Chapter Three

"You said you wanted to touch my chest," Alex said, licking his upper lip. "Is that right?"

We were sitting on the white leather sofa in his living room. Beyond the windows that surrounded us, the Manhattan skyline twinkled and gleamed, not unlike his turquoise eyes, which met mine with a disarming intensity I hadn't seen in them before. He seemed different to me. Almost primal.

"I do," I said, but as much as I did, my voice nevertheless sounded uncertain. I felt slightly light-headed because I knew what was about to happen. Having sex after so many years of waiting wouldn't just change my life. It also would change my relationship with Alex, and that frightened me.

What if I didn't please him in bed? What if I was too frigid, despite feeling like parts of me were on fire at that moment? He had been married before. Regardless of what Blackwell said, he must have had experiences with other women. Were any of them virgins, like me? I doubted it. Would he be gentle? Looking at him now, at the way his unwavering stare was feasting on me, that seemed unlikely.

He moved closer to me. "Then, why don't you do it? And why not start by removing my tie?"

He was close enough now that I could smell the faintest scent of his cologne, which somehow made me want him more because, like him, it was masculine. I reached out a hand to tug on his tie, and when I did, I surprised myself when I pulled it swiftly off him, casting it to the floor.

"That was quick."

"Sorry."

"Are you in a hurry?"

"I don't know." But I was. I knew I was. I was anxious to have him on top of me and inside of me, even though I knew there would be pain. Or would there be? I had no clue. Maybe he knew a way around the pain. Maybe he had a few tricks coming my way that would alleviate the pain. It was embarrassing that, at this point in my life, I had no idea what to expect other than what I'd heard from Lisa and a few other girlfriends. I felt pathetic.

"Unbutton my shirt, but don't do it quickly. Don't be in such a rush."

"I can't help myself."

"I don't care if you can't help yourself. Do it slowly. When it's time, I want you wet for me."

I already am wet.

"The top button," he said. There was a new note in his voice. Deeper. Rougher. When he spoke, it was a command. "Unbutton it."

I did as he said, exposing his throat.

"Keep going. One by one. That's right. Don't hurry."

"You're wearing a T-shirt."

"Of course I am. Otherwise, you'd see my skin beneath the shirt." He cocked his head at me. "Do you feel cheated?"

"In a way."

"Good. Now finish."

"You're going to have to stand," I said. "The rest of your shirt is tucked into your pants."

"So, it is."

The trace of a smile crossed his lips, but only fleetingly. He stood, tapped my feet apart with his shoes, and moved directly in front of me. And then I saw the reason for the smile. His excitement was clearly visible in his pants, and it now was only inches

Annihilate Me 2 33

from my face. He put his hands on his hips and looked down at me when I looked up at him.

"The shirt, Jennifer. Why don't you focus on that instead? You'll see the rest of the package later. Untuck my shirt. Unbutton it. Wait for me to tell you what to do next."

He was being dominant with me, but, despite my past with my father, I somehow didn't mind it. It was sexy, actually something of a turn-on, so I went with it. When I had the chance later, I'd just take control of the situation and do the same to him—once I knew what the hell I was doing. But for the moment, I didn't. So I did as I was told, but when I lifted his shirt so I could finish unbuttoning it, I also lifted a portion of his T-shirt and revealed a trace of tanned flesh before the shirt fell back to conceal it.

"You did that on purpose," he said.

"No, I didn't."

"Why don't I believe that?"

"I don't know. It's true."

"I wonder if it is. Did you like what you saw?"

"I—"

"Just unbutton the shirt. Then stand."

I did.

"Take off my jacket."

I removed it and then pressed the fabric against my nose. With his eyes fixed on mine, I breathed in deeply before tossing the jacket onto the sofa. The act of that gesture seemed to inflame him for a moment, but then he tamped it down. "To remove my shirt, you'll need to unbutton the cuffs. Focus, Jennifer."

I did as I was told, and then I gently pulled the shirt off him. I knew he was in shape, but not in this kind of shape. His chest appeared full and firm, bulky and rock hard beneath the T-shirt. I could see the corded muscles in his abdomen, and his arms were bigger than I thought they'd be. I usually only saw him in a jacket of some sort. The only exception was the night he arrived at the restaurant in casual clothes. But then it was dark and the shirt he wore fit loosely. Looking at him now, I could see that his nipples were as hard as my own. The shirt fit so snugly that little was left to the imagination. And then, in a surprising gesture, he didn't allow me to finish undressing him. In one quick motion, he pulled the T-shirt over his head and stood bare-chested in front of me.

"There's your chest," he said in a deep voice. "Do you still want to touch it?"

I admired it before I spoke. "I do."

"What if I told you that wasn't allowed tonight? What if I told you that it was only me who was going to touch you?"

I looked at him. "Why would you do that?"

"Because I might want to."

I looked at his chest, which was muscled and lightly hairy in the most appealing way. Starting just beneath his pecs ran a thin line of hair that rippled over his ridiculous abs and disappeared into the well of his pants. God only knew what awaited me there. His nipples were taut and erect. I don't know why, but I wanted to put my mouth on them. I wanted to flick my tongue over them and maybe bite them. But he wouldn't let me touch him, which was too much. I decided to go for it, anyway. I reached out to touch him, but before I could, he firmly pressed me down on to the sofa.

"What do you want, Jennifer?"

I was dizzy with lust. "I want you."

"How badly do you want me?"

"Like I've never wanted anyone else before."

"Why?"

"Because I feel connected to you. Safe with you. And I want you."

I saw him look at my martini, which I'd barely touched. I felt that he looked at it to see if I'd had too much to drink and wasn't thinking clearly. But I was. I'd only had a few sips.

"I'm not going through with this if it's just about taking your virginity."

"That's not what this is about."

"What is it, then?"

I was so filled with desire and anticipation. It was a challenge just to think. "I want to be with you, Alex. I want you inside of me. Please. I can't take much more of this."

"Much more of what?"

"You. Standing in front of me like that. The tension. I can't stand it much longer."

"I'm not going to take you unless you belong to me."

"Unless I what?"

"I want you to be mine."

"What are you talking about?"

"I want you to commit to being my girlfriend, or this isn't happening. I'm not going to take your virginity if this is just a curiosity. I won't do that to you because you deserve better. I need to make sure that you know what you are doing, and that you know how far I might take this."

"What do you mean? How far *will* you take this?"

"Just answer the question. I need to know from you that I'm the one, or this isn't going to happen. I can't do that to you. Your first time should be special. You're not some sixteen-year-old girl who doesn't know what she's doing. You know exactly what you're doing and how this will change us. You've held back for years for a reason. Obviously, you've been waiting for the right man. I need you to be sure that I'm that man."

"You are."

"Will you be exclusive to me?"

I screwed up my face at him. "Is that even a question? Of course I will. Don't you know me by now? Why would you ask such a thing?"

"Because exclusivity is a loaded term for me."

"I don't understand."

He leaned down toward my ear, the stubble on his chin once again sending me to the edge when it brushed against my earlobe. When he spoke, it was a whisper. "Then let me explain. I want to do things to you that are so intimate, only we share them. You'll never know when I want to take you. It could be in my car, at my office, at a restaurant, here on the floor, in any one of my homes, or in any number of other places. Maybe even in public. I am not exactly vanilla when it comes to sex, Jennifer. I never have been. I like to experiment—a lot. I've been celibate for four years, ever since my wife died. Like you, I've also waited for that one special person. The only person. I knew I found her that night at the Four Seasons. I knew it when I became jealous of the attention you were receiving. I'm not usually a jealous man, but I was that night, and it was for a good reason. And then I fucked everything up when I mistreated you. Before we go forward, I need to make sure that you do feel safe with me, that you mean it when you say that you feel safe with me. I need to know that you seriously want to be with me, and that you will trust in me in the process."

"What process?"

"You'll see."

"You're being so vague."

"If you trust me, that shouldn't matter."

"I do trust you."

"Then we'll take it slowly," he said. "Hand me my shirt."

I looked at him in confusion.

"This isn't happening tonight," he said.

"What are you talking about?"

"I want this to build even more than it has."

"Why?"

"This is why."

In one fluid motion, he was on his knees and pressing my legs apart. He leaned into me, curved his hands around the low of my back and kissed me hard on the mouth. Gently, he cupped my breasts while his tongue probed so deep that I lost myself in the moment and gave everything I had back to him.

I reached out to feel his chest. He moved my hands aside, but I was damned if I wasn't going to touch him, so I swatted him away and ran my hands along his rock-hard pecs and his silky torso. When I went for his nipples and pressed them hard between my fingers, he caught his breath and pulled away from me with a look of surprise and raw passion. His chest and torso were covered in little red indentations from the crystals sewn into my dress. I couldn't help a smile.

"I've branded you," I said.

He furrowed his brow as if he didn't understand.

"Look at your stomach."

He saw the marks, and then he looked back at me. "So you have. And who better to do so?"

He came toward me again and pushed further into me, sending me back on the sofa to the point that I could feel him against my knee, which sent rivers of excitement through me. He took my face in his hands and kissed me on the lips before he lowered his head to my neck, kissed me there, and then went to my swollen breasts, which were pressed tight against my dress. For a moment, he just admired them. Then, with a quick glance at me, he kissed each nipple, giving each a tiny bite that nearly made me come before he pulled me to my feet and cast me out of the moment.

"My shirt," he said.

"Why are you doing this?"

"I've told you. I want it to build. And it will build, to the point that neither of us knows what hit us. I'm also punishing myself for how I treated you before. And believe me, not being with you tonight is a punishment."

"But we're beyond that."

"Maybe one of us is. Maybe the other can't forgive himself for it. Would you like to finish your martini?"

"Only if you pour yourself into it."

He laughed at that. "I don't think there's any part of me that would fit in it. Shirt, please."

Reluctantly, I handed it to him. "Do you want the jacket and tie, too?"

"No. Just the shirt." He shrugged it on and buttoned it up, concealing everything that I fantasized about and wanted.

"I think you're cruel."

"You won't when I have my way with you."

"And when will that be?"

"No idea. Time will tell. We'll know when it's the right moment."

"Now is the right moment."

"No, it isn't."

"How can you say that?"

"Because I'm right."

"According to you."

"Can I see you tomorrow?"

"I have to work tomorrow."

"Then I'll be there to pick you up. We can come back here."

"Why? So you can tease me more?"

"Likely. Would you like that?"

"I can't believe this."

He smiled warmly at me. "Neither can I."

"You're frustrating me."

"I'm frustrating myself. I want you right now in ways that I've only wanted one other woman. But that was years ago. This is different."

"How is it different?"

"I never thought I'd be here again. But I am. And I'm not taking you until you're mine."

"I don't know how I'm going to sleep tonight or how I'm going to stay focused at work tomorrow."

"You think it's going to be any easier for me? That's the whole point of this. I'm punishing myself for what I did to you."

"But you're also punishing me."

"You'll see that I'm right. Let's give this time. Let's let it build."

I moved to speak, but he came forward and kissed me on the forehead, then on the lips before he moved his mouth to my ear. The stubble again—rough against my skin. Damn him. "Trust me on this, OK? You'll see. In the meantime, I'm hardly going to keep my hands off you. Or my mouth. Or my tongue. But I am going to make certain that your first time blows you away, Jennifer. When it happens, your body will experience things that you didn't know it was capable of experiencing. Or achieving. And then, when it becomes clear to you, you'll realize exactly why I'm doing this."

"Kiss me again."

But he didn't. Instead, he moved away from me. "I'll have a car waiting at the curb for you. The driver will make sure you get home safe. And I'll see you tomorrow night, OK?"

Bastard. "Fine," I said.

"The bathroom is just off to the right." He cracked a smile. "Before you leave, you might want to check your hair and makeup."

CHAPTER FOUR

In the back of the limousine, I rolled down the window next to me and breathed in the city in an effort to ease my nerves. I felt, at once, charged and cheated, turned on and angry. I was riding on the cold rails of whatever control I had left, which wasn't much. *He's going to be the end of me*, I thought. *Why did he stop that from happening?*

In my clutch, I felt my cell buzz. I reached for it, clicked it on, and knew it was a text of some sort from Alex. But it wasn't a text. It was an email. The subject line simply said, "For you. And only for you. No one else."

Attached was a photograph. I downloaded it, and when I saw what it was, my hand absentmindedly went to my breast. He'd taken a photo of himself in his bathroom mirror. His shirt was off, as was his T-shirt. On his face was a smirk. His chest and abs were bared to me. It was too much—an absolute tease—but two could play this game. I wasn't about to be undone.

I asked the driver for privacy, and the privacy glass went up between us.

How best to get to Alex? What could I do to top that photo? I thought about it for a moment, and then I leaned forward and unzipped the back of my dress. I let the top fall into my lap and expose my breasts, which were covered with the sexy lace bra Blackwell chose for me earlier.

My hands started to tremble at the thought of what I was about to do. I strategically parted my hair behind me and placed it over my breasts in a way that I knew would turn him on.

I'd never done anything like this, but for whatever reason and regardless of how hard my heart was beating, I wanted to do it. I pressed back against the cool leather seat, turned the phone around so the camera faced me, and took several shots of myself either staring intently into the lens or with my lips slightly parted and my eyes closed. The camera's flash lit the inside of the limousine with several small explosions of light. I could only imagine what the driver was thinking, or if he could even see through the dark glass. But I decided I didn't care. Let him think what he wanted. I was going to give Alex exactly what he deserved. I dipped my head back, as if I was in the throes of an orgasm, and took more photos.

When I was finished, I couldn't help a giggle. I'd never been that free with my body. And better yet, it felt right.

Before I pulled my dress back up, I looked at the pictures, most of which I disliked, with the exception of one. One was perfect. It showed just enough skin as well as part of the lace on my bra. My hair, which I knew he loved when I wore it down, curved over my breasts, which were full and round, the cleavage deep. In the photo, I was biting my lower lip. My eyes were closed and my head was pressed back against the leather seat as if there was something inside of me that needed to get out—which was true enough. I thought I looked kind of hot, which was fitting since inside, I was boiling over. I looked at the photo again and couldn't help another giggle.

Obviously, I've lost it.

But so be it. I attached the photo in a return email to him, and wrote in the subject line, "This right here? This is what you're missing." Before I could even think about what I'd done and thus stop myself, I pressed the send button. I shook my head at the audacity of my actions, and then I quickly pulled myself together. When I moved to zip up the back of my dress, I became aware that I was so turned on, I was wet again.

And then my cell buzzed. This time it was indeed a text.

"You aren't going to make this easy for me, are you?"

I raised my eyebrows at that, and shot him a text. "I'm just following your lead. And by the way, you'll never know when I'll email you a similar photo, so be prepared. It could be while you're at work. At one of your events. Or maybe even during a meeting. In fact, maybe the latter is the best choice given what you cheated me out of tonight."

I waited a moment, and he rang in again. "I can always ask the driver to turn the car around, you know?"

I thought about that. But as much as I wanted him, I rejected the idea. What was happening between us was driving me crazy with excitement, but now I saw the logic in the statement he'd made earlier. Let it build to the point that neither of us can stand it any longer. Then, when the time is right, what we'll experience together should be something that neither of us will forget.

It'll be mind blowing.

"Sorry," I wrote. "But you had your chance. We're letting this build. Maybe a few months?"

I pressed the send button, and awaited a new text from him. When it came, this one said, "Not months, Ms. Kent."

"I'm thinking several months. You shouldn't have done that to me."

"I did what I felt was right."

"Is your shirt back on?"

"I'm not wearing anything. Would you like a photo of that?"

I blushed when I read that post, and closed my eyes at the thought of it. "I can wait. Sort of."

"Are we sexting?"

"I believe we are."

"Have you ever sexted before?"

"I think you know better."

"Neither have I. You'd think we were a couple of teenagers."

"That's funny," I wrote. "I feel like a woman."

* * *

When the driver dropped me at my apartment, I thanked him, ran across the dimly lit street, and quickly stuck my key in the door. I couldn't wait to get out of this neighborhood. It was dark, it was sketchy, and it gave me the creeps. I had a steady income now. There was no longer an excuse to stay here. Lisa and I needed to find something soon.

Only when I was safely inside did I hear the driver pull away.

I climbed the four flights of stairs and entered the apartment. Lisa sat across the room, the pages of a manuscript in her hand and her nightly martini next to her. She glanced up at me when I stepped inside and said hello before circling something on the manuscript. She then dropped it in her lap and just looked at me.

"Well, well," she said. "Look at you."

I put my clutch and cell down onto the kitchen counter. I could hide nothing from Lisa. She'd be on to me in a second. In fact, she was on to me now. "Whatever do you mean?"

She picked up her martini and took a sip. There was mischief in her eyes when she said, "Lovely dress."

"Thank you. It's supposed to evoke *Gatsby*."

"You don't say?"

"That was the idea."

"A rousing success." She looked down at my feet. "Pretty shoes."

"I like them."

"Are they comfortable?"

"No blisters for me today."

"At least not on your feet."

"Excuse me?"

"Nothing. Just mumbling. Those are some jewels."

"You think?"

"Mmm-hmm. Oh, and I assume that you went out tonight with some makeup on? And that your hair wasn't the hot mess that it is right now? And that you didn't go out in public with any stains on your dress? You know, like that one right there."

She pointed at my crotch.

I looked down and—mortified—I saw the stain.

"Oh, my God. This dress cost a fortune."

"Girl, you're in a hot state of disrepair."

I came into the living area and sat on the sofa.

"Don't you think you should put down a towel before you sit on that sofa?"

"Oh, please."

"No, really. Please."

"Whatever." I leaned back against the sofa and grinned up at the ceiling.

"Should I leave you alone?"

"Oh, no. We're going to talk. I'm on fire. You have no idea."

"Oh, I think I'm getting the picture. Did he give you a hickey?"

"Do he give me a what?"

"A hickey."

"Nobody gives me a hickey. No one even uses that word anymore."

"Just teasing. But I have to say that it's a relief that you still have your restraint. That's good."

"You don't even know how much restraint I showed tonight."

"Looking at you, I'd guess that you showed none."

"Not true. I was a ball of restraint, even if it wasn't by choice."

"So, you're still as pure as bottled water?"

"I wouldn't go that far. Let's just say I'm... intact."

She put her drink on the table beside her and stretched her hands behind her. She was so petite, it was as if she was barely there. "All right," she said. "I need the deets. Spill them. Enough of this silliness.

I've been dying to hear all night how your evening went, and it looks as if you two got along swimmingly, so to speak. Thus the towel I wished for earlier."

"Very funny. That has never happened to me before. I hope I haven't ruined the dress. It cost a fortune."

"You'll be fine. Take it to a good dry cleaner, and they'll get the stain out. Though I wouldn't want to be you when you have to point it out to them."

"What am I going to say to them?"

"Nothing. They'll know what it is, and judgment will thunder down upon you. Just look contrite, grab your ticket, and get the hell out of there." She pulled her blonde hair behind her head. Beside her, the air conditioner hummed. "So, are you going to tell me what happened or not?"

"You are not going to be prepared for any of it."

"Jennifer, you look as if you've been roughed up by a dozen thugs, but in the best way. And your eyes are a little unfocused, which isn't like you, except for when you've had a bit too much to drink, which I've witnessed a few times too many. But I doubt that's the case here. And I *am* prepared. Minus the dress, the shoes, and the jewels, I think I've been where you are now. Only several years ago. It was heaven and hell, all at once." She tucked her legs beneath her, but then she untucked them and stood. "What am I thinking? You need a martini. That will loosen you up enough to talk. I want the good shit. Be right back."

"Do we have good vodka?"

"You know we do. We can afford it now. What's wrong with you?"

"I think I have amnesia."

"Sweetie, you're just horny. You're a vessel of pulsing hormones. It'll pass. Let me get you a drink. It'll numb the pain. Or whatever it is your going through."

"That would be a mystery," I said.

Then I told her about the facts of my night.

* * *

"He did what?"

"You heard me."

"And you did what?"

"You heard me."

"I can't believe this. Who are you?"

"I don't know anymore."

"Let me see the photos."

"Oh, come on."

"We share everything. Do you really expect me not to ask to see them? Come on, Jennifer! You can't give me a blow-by-blow like that and expect me not to ask to see the photos."

"Fine. But let's just say it's not my proudest moment."

"Who cares? For you to trust someone like that says it all to me. I said it earlier and I'll say it again— you're in deep. I just didn't realize how deep."

I got my phone and brought up the photograph he sent. I showed it to her. Greedily, she took my cell from my hand.

"Holy shit. I've seen photos of him online, but not like this. He's hotter than I thought. Look at that chest, never mind his abs. As busy as he is, where does he find time to stay in that kind of shape? And look at that smirk on his face. You know, if my apocalyptic zombie books ever get made into a movie, I'd want the lead actor to look like him. Or, frankly, to be him."

"I don't think Alex acts."

"But I bet he could finance the project. I've done my research. Part of Wenn is Wenn Entertainment!"

"You're killing me."

She looked at his photo again, and sighed. "He's totally into this." She looked up in approval. "Good for you, sweetie. Really. Now, where's that photo of you?"

"You don't want to see that."

"Oh, yes, I do."

"Just swipe to the next image then."

She did. I winced. And then, for whatever reason, she was silent for a moment. I'd gone too far. I knew it. But then she said, "Hello, Victoria's Secret supermodel. Look at you. And tasteful, too. Nice bit of cleavage. Love the hair covering the boobs, but just showing a trace of lace. And you're biting your lip, your eyes are closed, and your head is pressed back. It's obvious you're in the back of a limo. This must have slayed him. Well played, love. Well played. It's as if Mario Testino took this shot, only with a Warhol edge."

"Mario who?"

"You wouldn't understand."

"Is he one of your fashion photographers?"

"He's one of the fashion photographers. Think Madonna, Madonna, Madonna—throughout the years. And many other famous women." She admired the photo a moment more before handing me back my cell. "I bet that made Alex second guess everything."

"After he received it, he wanted to ask the driver to turn the limo around. I told him that wasn't happening because I think he's right. This should build. I want it to build."

"Are we building a two-story home? Or a skyscraper?"

"Definitely not a skyscraper."

"Well, that's good."

"But I will wait as long as it takes for it to feel right."

"When it does happen, you better be ready for that, honey. Because this man is going to annihilate you."

"Is that one of your zombie words?"

She finished her martini and cocked her head at me. "Maybe. But when he gets his hands on you and you both decide the moment is right? That's what's going to happen. You're going to feel annihilated, but in the best sense. He's going to rid you of your virginity, and destroy you in bed. Those are the two definitions of 'annihilate': 'rid' and 'destroy.' Just you wait and see."

CHAPTER FIVE

The next morning at six, my cell rang. I'd left it on my bedside table in case Alex called during the night, which he hadn't. I reached for it, and saw his name on the screen when I answered.

"Mr. Wenn," I said.

"Ms. Kent."

"How are you this morning?"

"Despite getting no sleep? Surprisingly good."

"What kept you from sleep?" I asked.

"What do you think? Did you sleep?"

"There might have been some tossing and turning."

"Just the tossing and turning?"

"What are you implying?"

"That you did something to give yourself relief."

"What if I did?" I said.

"Did you?"

"No."

"Would you judge me if I did?"

"I thought this was about holding back," I said.

"It is. I did nothing to myself last night, though I sure as hell wanted to. I was hard for a good hour."

I blushed at the thought. "It was your choice."

"It was the right choice. By the way, that was an interesting photo you took of yourself last night. And an unexpected one."

"I could say the same."

"Do you ever take a bad photograph?"

"I've taken my share of them."

"I doubt that," I said. "I think I looked at you for most of the night."

"I hope your battery held out."

"Miraculously, it did."

"Look," he said. "I know you have to work tonight, but it's still early and my first meeting isn't until nine. Are you up for breakfast?"

It would take me forty-five minutes to get ready. "I'd love to have breakfast with you. Where should I meet you?"

"At my place. I'm cooking."

"You cook?"

"I do."

What doesn't he do?

"When should I send a car for you?"

"At seven?"

"That'll only give us a couple of hours...."

"But we'll have tonight, after I get out of work."

"I have an event tonight," he said. "It's a big one, so I'll probably be too late to pick you up. But a car will be waiting for you to make sure you get home safely. I apologize."

"There's no need to apologize. You need to tend to your business, Alex."

He sounded frustrated when he said, "I also need to see you more than just a couple of hours a day, Jennifer."

I wasn't about to engage him now. He worked days and evenings, and I worked evenings. What did he expect? I had two days off a week, with an additional day off to try out new restaurants for Stephen. Somehow, if he wanted to see more of me, Alex would have to adjust his schedule, if that was even possible, which it should be since he owned Wenn. But I knew better. That wouldn't be so easy for him to do. The board at Wenn expected a lot from him, including attending as many events as possible. Getting away so we could see each other was going to be an issue. *And how is that going to affect our relationship?*

"We're wasting time," I said. "Let me take a shower. Send the car sooner than later. I'll be ready before you know it."

* * *

When I arrived at Wenn ten minutes before seven, the driver told me to go to Mr. Wenn's private elevator. "Someone will be waiting there for you. They'll see to it that you have access, Ms. Kent."

"Thank you," I said.

I went inside, and was greeted by the security guards at the front desk, all of whom addressed me by name, which felt bizarre to me. I nodded at them as I went to the concealed elevator just behind them. When I did, I saw that the person who was waiting for me was Alex himself. He was in jeans and a T-shirt, but otherwise was perfectly groomed and ready to start the day as soon as he changed into his suit. He took me in his arms and kissed me when I walked over to him.

"You're here early," he said.

"I'm curious to see how well you cook."

"Is that it?"

"It depends on how we define 'cooking'?"

"Breakfast."

"Oh, that."

"Yes, that."

"That's fine. And maybe I came because I wanted to spend more time with you."

"That makes me happy," he said. And I could tell that it did, even though there was an undercurrent I couldn't quite define. He seemed distracted again, just as he had early last night, before I came clean with him about my past and things took a romantic turn. I decided to just be myself, and see how the next two hours played out, especially considering what had happened between us the night before. Would the chemistry still be there? Or was all of that just in the heat of the moment? I hoped it wasn't, but what did I know?

He slid a card into a slot next to the elevator and we stepped inside when the doors opened. When they shut, the elevator soared, and he pressed me against the rear wall. "You look beautiful," he said, kissing me on the neck and then hard on the lips before he leaned me back and fingered the length of my hair. "And your hair is curly."

"No time for a flat iron this morning."

"I like it when it's like this. It reminds me of the first time we met."

"Why does that seem like ages ago?"

"It's only happened to me once before, but, sometimes when you meet someone, it's as if you've known that person forever."

Was he referring to his wife? Of course he was. I wondered what she was like and what she had looked like. Though I'd looked, I'd seen no photographs of her in his apartment the night before. Maybe they were too much for him to look at. Perhaps they were gone for a reason—so he could move on with his life. Regardless of whatever was happening between us now, I felt terrible that he lost his wife so early. It must have devastated him.

The elevator slowed, he took my hand, and we stepped out. It was so sunny—and his apartment was so white—that the light streaming through the surround of windows was almost blinding.

"How can you stand that?" I asked.

"Let's just say it's an instant wake-up call."

"I bet it works."

He smiled. "Have you ever been to Paris?" he asked when we left the elevator.

"So far, I've gotten as far as Manhattan."

"Not a bad start. Do you like French food?"

"I love it. Along the coast in Maine, there are a few very good French restaurants."

"I miss Maine."

"I don't."

He glanced at me, but said nothing. "Do you think you'll be taking me to any French restaurants in New York?"

"If any hot new ones open up, it'll be my pleasure. What other kinds of food do you like?"

"It doesn't matter, Jennifer. As rare as they seem they're going to be, a night out with you is what matters to me."

He tightened his grip on my hand, but I couldn't help but linger on what he really was saying. Because of the job I took and because of his own hectic schedule, our lives weren't designed for us to spend much time together. The undercurrent I sensed earlier was now clear. Not being together was going to be difficult for him, possibly because his wife, who might not have worked, had always been available to him. And if I was honest, it also was going to be difficult on me. So, where did that leave us now? How would the reality of our situations impact what was only a budding relationship? At this point, everything was so fragile, it was as if we were walking on broken glass. Leaving him now would be difficult, but not as difficult as it would if months had passed. If we invested in each other for a long period of time, it would tear my heart out if we finally decided we couldn't be together because of mere conflicts in our schedules. But we each had our own lives to live. He didn't have to worry about his next meal or the next month's rent—I did. So, which would win out? The potential for a meaningful relationship or work?

I had a feeling that too often in this particular city—by far one of the most aggressive and challenging of cities—it was work and that saddened me.

"How about an omelet with fresh tarragon, salt, and pepper beaten into the eggs, roasted asparagus tucked inside, and a bit of Parmesan cheese on top? Fresh orange juice, obviously. And a croissant and good coffee?"

"Are you sure you haven't ordered in?"

"With the exception of the croissants, I'm positive. You'll witness all of it."

"It sounds fabulous, but do you have time to make all of that?"

"It's quicker than it sounds. That's what I love about French food. Some of it is time consuming to prepare, but much of it is actually simple because they don't use a lot of ingredients. It's all about the preparation and the execution—in this case, you cook the eggs very slowly. Protein should be cooked on the lowest heat for the tenderest results. When I was growing up, our cook, Michelle, who is French, taught me a lot. To escape from my mother, which I did as often as possible for reasons I won't bore you with, I spent a lot time with Michelle in the kitchen. I enjoyed learning from her because she was kind to me, because she loved me, and because I could hide when I was with her. She was an amazing chef. Sometimes, I think she had more influence on me than my mother. She was a sweet, loving woman, but stern when she needed to be. 'Not like that, Alex—like this. Pay attention. You're making too much of it. Why do you harm the food like that? You should love it. Caress it. It's not that difficult, mon chéri. Treat it like a woman. You'll see what I mean. Yes, that's right. Just like that.' That sort of thing."

Why did he need to escape from his mother? "I would love to meet Michelle. Is she still alive?"

"She is, but she's in a nursing home. Parkinson's. She doesn't know me anymore, but I visit as often as I can anyway. I just like being near her. I wish she was well enough to know you, but in her condition, that's impossible." His throat thickened when he spoke, but he quickly cleared it. Wherever she was, I had no question that he was taking care of her. "Let's go to the kitchen. Sit at the bar. You're the business junky. Read the paper. I'll do the rest."

"Can't I help?"

"Not at all. You're my guest." He raised his eyebrows at me. "Maybe one day you'll cook breakfast for me."

"Shakespeare never came up with more tragic words."

He shook his head at me, but I could feel his affection. "Oh, come on."

"I can do frozen waffles and toast. And coffee. I totally can do coffee."

"So, you don't cook?"

"Well, not at the level you're about to cook, and certainly not French. But I am a good homestyle cook. I can cook like my grandmother used to cook for me. It's very rustic, but delicious, if you like that sort of thing, which I do. I can make a killer apple pie. And I know how to make a good steak. As an additional bonus, roasted chicken and vegetables are a snap for me. I've got those covered."

"I remember having lunches and dinners with my friends when I was a boy summering in Maine. None of it was stuffy—but all of it was good."

"*That* I can do for you, Alex."

"When it gets colder, can you make a good beef stew?"

"Absolutely. And a chicken soup that will curl your toes. And obviously fish—I can do any sort of fish, and it always will be tender for the same reason those eggs you're cooking will be. Low, low heat. Oh, and I can do a macaroni and cheese with fresh mushrooms, lobster, and spinach that you'll never forget. And I have a bit more up my sleeve. Just not the super fancy stuff you're about to do."

"I'm so glad you're here, Jennifer."

We went into the kitchen, which was a massive space filled with high-end appliances, a large bar area with comfortable stools, lots of overhead lighting, and the aroma of fresh coffee.

"Would you like a cup?"

"I'm dying for a cup."

"Cream? Sugar?"

"Both, please."

Before he poured the coffee into a large white mug, he put out a tray service. "Help yourself."

I went straight for the cream and sugar, and indulged. He watched me with a smile. The coffee was delicious. After getting almost no sleep, I was thankful for it.

And I knew I was damned lucky for him. I watched him move around the kitchen, which seemed like a lover to him. He knew exactly where everything was. I watched him chop the tarragon and lightly beat the eggs with a bit of heavy cream in a glass bowl. He prepared the asparagus with olive oil and salt for roasting, and ground the fresh Parmesan in a food processor so it could be used later. The croissants looked divine and flaky beneath the domed pastry dish. Butter softened to room temperature sat beside them. Next to the croissants were two white plates, silverware, napkins, and two juice glasses. The *Times* was to my right.

I opened it to the business section while he cooked. I scanned the page and was surprised to find a story with a headline that read "Wenn Eyes Kobus Airlines." It was a brief story that detailed the troubled airline and how its fleet could benefit the successful Wenn Air. When asked if the rumors were true, Wenn declined comment, though the *Times* reported that several unnamed sources confirmed that Wenn did plan to go forward with a takeover bid. Gordon Kobus, who owned the airline, did comment. I remembered him from the fundraising gala at the Museum of Natural History where he stared with open hostility at Alex while we were in the Theodore

Roosevelt Rotunda. The man gave me the creeps. His quote gave me a chill: "Alexander Wenn's father once wanted my airline, and he failed to take it away from me. So will his son, who isn't half the businessman his father was. He's a mere boy. It won't happen. Mr. Wenn can rest assured of that. I will fight him and the board of Wenn Enterprises every step of the way should they come anywhere near Kobus."

"That's just a damned threat," I said aloud.

Alex put the asparagus in the oven and looked up at me. "You found the story, I see."

"Who leaked it?"

He shrugged. "Somebody did. It might have been Kobus himself."

"Because his stock would soar on such news."

"That's right."

"I hope it didn't come from in-house."

"I'll never know. The board is behind the idea, so I'm thinking it didn't come from anyone within Wenn. I'm thinking Kobus wanted his stock to rise on the news. As for the 'unnamed sources,' I have no clue who they could be."

I decided to go there. "Last night, you seemed distracted when you picked me up. This morning, I felt the same way when I saw you. I'm assuming this is why."

"It isn't."

"Then, what's troubling you?"

He reached for an oven timer and set it for the asparagus. "I want to spend more time with you, but I can already see that going forward that's going to be difficult. Sometimes it's going to be impossible. That worries me. And it frustrates me because I don't see an end to it. I know you have your commitments, as I do, but to give this our best shot, I see only one solution, which I'm fairly certain you won't take."

"What's that?"

"I want you to come back to Wenn," he said. "As soon as possible and in whatever capacity you wish. You love business. I can offer you the world of big business. If you agree, I'll know for certain that we can spend time together because I'll make that a priority."

I started to speak, but he interrupted. "Just let me get breakfast going, or my reputation for being a halfway decent cook is going to be blown, which Michelle would have my ass for. We'll talk after we eat. I'll listen to you and I'll hear you, but I hope that we can work something out, Jennifer. I've always been decisive about what I want. I didn't take asking you to be my girlfriend lightly. I asked you because that is exactly what I wanted, and what I continue to want. *You* are who I want. I know this has happened very quickly—I get it—but maybe it has for a reason. Having you here now feels right to me. It feels like this is how it should be. I know I'm probably way ahead of you in terms of our relationship, but that's just who I am, so I'm being honest with you. After we eat, we'll talk. OK?"

My head was spinning, and I could feel my guard going up. I liked my job at db Bistro. I won that job on my own merits, which was important to me. But I couldn't deny his point, and I also worried about how the lack of seeing each other would affect our relationship. Of course it would. We'd rarely see each other. I wasn't a fool—things would collapse because of that. But I never saw this job offer coming, and I wasn't sure what to make of it. Still, I had to at least hear him out and give it some thought. It was only the right thing to do.

"OK," I said. "We'll eat, and then we'll talk."

CHAPTER SIX

"How were the eggs?" Alex asked, looking at my empty plate.

I wiped my mouth with a napkin, and shot him a glance. "Is that even a question?"

He smiled at me, and when he did, his eyes were soft.

"They were heaven. All of it was. Michelle trained you very well." I checked my watch. "We probably should talk. It's fifteen minutes before eight, and your meeting is at nine. Living room?"

"Sure. Another cup of coffee?"

"I'd love another. Let me help you clean up."

He tried to say no, but already I was out of my seat. I stacked the plates, separated the silverware, and cradled the two empty juice glasses around the bar to the sink. I rinsed off everything while he stood beside me and poured the coffee. I thought about what he said earlier about this feeling right to him. Helping him in the kitchen felt natural to me. It was the oddest thing. I'd only known this man for a few weeks, but there was a rhythm between us that was undeniable. And confusing. I was too new to all of this, and had to wonder if what was happening between us was special, or if it was as rare as he suggested it was.

Lisa will know.

When we finished in the kitchen, the tension between us was high because neither of us knew what was going to be said. But he still reached for my hand when we walked into the living room with our coffee. I could tell that he was nervous, so I squeezed back. We sat on the white leather sofa, put our mugs down on the coffee table, and Alex reached for my legs and swung them over his lap. He removed my sandals and started to rub my feet.

"I know you love your job, Jennifer. And I know that it's important to you that you landed it on your own. You have every reason to be proud of that. I'm proud of you for it."

I didn't say anything at first—I just watched him. He wasn't looking at me. Instead, he had a brooding look on his face as he focused on my feet. He was impossibly handsome and kind, regardless of the rougher, more dominant side I'd seen in him last night. And I didn't want this to end, just as I didn't want to shortchange my career. Wenn could offer me opportunities that I wouldn't receive at db Bistro. Obviously. But what was he proposing? Earlier, he said anything I wanted. But I wanted something that complemented my skills. I wasn't about to take anything more than that. If I did, I would regret it, and it would cheapen everything that was blossoming between us.

"That night with Cyrus," I said. "I didn't enjoy the end of the night, to say the least, but I did enjoy strategizing with you on how best to work a potential deal. I don't want to sound arrogant, but I know that because of me, you landed that deal with Stavros Shipping."

He looked up me. "You think I don't know that? You were instrumental. Even the board knows it. I told them what you did."

I didn't know that. He could have taken the credit for himself, but he didn't. I felt a rush of affection for him then. But then I checked myself, and focused on my future.

"If I did this, I'd only consider a job that I had earned. I don't want any handouts just so we can be together. I want to be valued for my contributions, and not like I'm there only because I'm Alexander Wenn's companion."

"Girlfriend."

"Companion. I know you keep saying girlfriend, but I'm not there yet. Still, as I promised last night, I *will* be exclusive to you. I've never been in a relationship before. I need to see how this unfolds, and I need for you to respect that it might take longer for me to say that word than it took you. It seemed so easy for you."

"It *was* easy for me. You're not the first woman of interest to come along since my wife died, Jennifer. I think you've seen a slice of what I have to deal with when I go out. Since Diana's death, I haven't called anyone my girlfriend until I met you because I haven't dated anyone. I said it for a reason. It's what I want. It's what's in my heart. I know this is right."

"I just need time, Alex. I need to let it build in a different way. Not just sexually. Though that wasn't so bad last night, as you clearly saw when I practically bumped into walls on my way out. But mentally and emotionally too. Does that make sense? I need it all before I can say that word."

"I'm just ahead of you, which is fine." He lifted my foot and kissed it before he started to rub it again. "Eventually, I'll get you there."

"Back to that night with Cyrus. I consulted you that night. I gave you an angle you hadn't considered. I think you've seen that when it comes to what's happening in the business world, I'm pretty much on top of it. I have good instincts and ideas. I think a good fit for me at Wenn would be as a consultant to you. Maybe to go to these events with you and meet the players. During the day, we could see each other in private and strategize about the next target. I think I could succeed at that. And because of the Stavros deal, which will make Wenn hundreds of millions, I think I've earned that. Better yet, I wouldn't feel as if I was just given something so we could be together. What matters to me is that I'm in a job in which I feel valued for my work and my contributions. How do you feel about that?"

"You'd like to be my consultant?" he asked.

"I think that would be a good fit. I think we could get some work done together."

"If I offered you the job now, would you take it?"

"We'd need to discuss salary first. A fair wage."

"What did you have in mind?"

"I have nothing in mind. So far, this has all been off the cuff. I was expecting breakfast, not this conversation."

"What are you worth, Jennifer? Don't lowball yourself. Tell me what you're worth."

I thought about it for a moment. I knew what other consultants made in the city. It often was an outrageous sum, well into seven figures. But I was only twenty-five, so I needed to scale it way back without underselling myself or what I'd already achieved for Wenn.

"At this point in my career and with what I've already done for you? Five hundred thousand a year, with bonuses for milestones achieved."

"Five hundred thousand?"

"That's right."

"I thought you were going to go for more."

"I'm here to work for a fair wage. Consulting the CEO of a major corporation for five hundred thousand a year is a fair wage in this city, especially considering my age and my experience. I'm not here to use our relationship for an inflated salary. It's not ethical."

"So, you see? This is one of the reasons I want to be with you. One of the many reasons. Others would have gone for much more. Others also wouldn't have given me the jewelry and the clothes back."

"I'm not like the others."

"I know you're not. Will you take the job?"

"I need to talk to Lisa about it. I share everything with her. She's *my* consultant. And if I take it, I'll need to give two weeks' notice at the restaurant. I will not leave Stephen in a bind. He and the rest of the staff have been good to me."

"That sounds more than fair. When do you think I'll have a definitive answer?"

"Once I talk to Lisa. At best, by the end of today. If not today, then sometime tomorrow. I think I might sleep on it."

"That works for me."

"Thank you."

And with that, he leaned me back on the sofa, and cupped my face in his hands, his eyes glinting with desire. He then went in for the kill for the next thirty minutes so that I was so spent, I barely could move when he gave me a final kiss and dashed into his bedroom to change into his suit.

After he'd changed, he came out of his bedroom and walked over to me. "I want you to have something," he said.

I was delusional. I looked at what he was holding out in his hand. It looked like a credit card. "What's that?"

"A key to the apartment."

"Isn't it a little too soon?"

"Look, Jennifer. Even if you don't take the job and we have to find out other ways to make this work, if you find yourself in this neighborhood and are in need of a place to unwind, even if I'm not here, I want you to know that you can do so here. It's not a big deal. I've already told security. They know who you are by name. You just need to say hello to them, walk past them, and use the place as if it's yours. Because it is yours. All of it. If you find that you need anything, just call the front desk and you'll have it in a flash. There's nothing you can't have, so just ask for it. OK?"

"Alex—"

"Jennifer, either way, we'll work this out."

"All right." I sat up and admired him. "I love you in a suit."

"You've said that before. Why?"

"Because you look handsome. Even when you're tie is crooked, as it is now."

I stood up and straightened it. I was so close to him, I could smell that damned cologne of his, which was faint but beyond sexy. It was never overpowering on him. Instead, he did it right and used it correctly. Cologne or perfume should only ever be an intimate experience. It should be part of one's essence, something someone else can smell only if they are very close to you. I kissed him full on the lips and thanked him for breakfast.

"I'm only a phone call away," he said. "Talk to Lisa. See what she thinks. If she's this close to you, I'd like to meet her soon. We three can have dinner together. Right here. I'll cook."

"There's no need for you to go to that kind of trouble. We can just go out."

"I'd rather stay in, if it's all the same. Cooking relaxes me. Seriously. It's what Michelle taught me. 'In the kitchen, you can become an artist,' she used to say to me. 'And when you become one, you lose yourself and your troubles will go away.'"

"She said that to you as a child?"

"She did."

"What troubles?"

He hesitated, but then said, "I didn't exactly have the happiest of childhoods. Michelle was acutely aware of that. She took me under her wing whenever she could. I suppose in many ways she protected me."

"From whom? Your mother? You mentioned her before in conjunction with Michelle."

"Yes, my mother. Often, my father too. But let's not discuss that now. Another time, OK?"

"OK."

"When Lisa comes for dinner, we'll have a few glasses of wine and I'll finally get to know your best friend. That's important to me. The people in your life are important to me. Whatever you want, I'll cook."

"Lisa is a total foodie."

"So this will be a test?"

"It will be to her."

"I'm up for the challenge."

"You'll need to be," I said.

"What I need to do is run."

"Have a good meeting."

He gave me a final kiss, and then he went for the elevator. "You as my consultant," he said inside the car. "I like that. And I think I need that. Thank you for considering it."

The doors swept shut, and then he was gone.

CHAPTER SEVEN

"**I**'ve been offered a job at Wenn," I said as I walked into our apartment. Lisa was on the sofa. On the table in front of her was a stack of manuscript pages. Soon, she'd ask me to proof her book. I couldn't wait to see what she'd created now. I was excited for her, and also for me because I loved her writing. Her stories scared the hell out me, but in a good way.

She put down her red pen, but didn't turn to look at me. "You've been offered what?"

"A job at Wenn."

"What time is it?"

"Just after ten. Why?"

"Mimosas," she said. "Two. And *tout suite*! I need to hear it all."

"I know we have a bottle of champagne. But do we even have orange juice?"

"I picked up a carton yesterday. I've got it covered."

"You often do," I said. How strong?"

"Just a taste of champagne—not too much. I have a day's worth of editing ahead of me, so my head needs to be clear. But right now, for the next hour or so, we are going to have a little chit-chat."

"That we are."

I made the drinks and brought her one in a fluted champagne glass.

"What a lovely color," she said, admiring the liquid in the glass.

"You and your zombies would like it more if the juice came from a blood orange."

"Sometimes I think you should be the writer, Jennifer. I'm totally stealing that."

"You can take from my lips whatever you want."

"Considering where you're lips are headed, that sounds dirty."

"You're impossible."

I sat down opposite her. The air conditioner whirred behind me and even though we were in the first days of September, it was still hot enough on the fourth floor of our prison camp of an apartment that the cool air felt like a bit of heaven to me. I remembered all those months ago, when we first arrived in Manhattan, and the hell we'd gone through over the summer because we couldn't afford an air conditioner. It had been awful, but we had worked through it, just as we'd worked through so many other problems together.

"Spill."

I told her about my breakfast with Alex, the conversation that ensued, and the job offer I now needed to weigh. "So, what do you think?" I asked.

"I saw this coming, but I sure as hell didn't see five hundred grand coming. You came up with the job and negotiated the price?"

"I did, but I wouldn't call it a negotiation. He just agreed to it. I probably could have asked for a million and I would have received it. But I'm not worth that. What I'm worth is five hundred thousand. Considering what I've already done for Wenn when it comes to Stavros Shipping, and especially considering what most consultants make in this city and in this business, that's a fair wage. I never would take advantage of him, and I know I can do the job."

"There will be a lot of expectations with that kind of money."

"I'm fine with that."

She smiled at me, and while I could tell that she was happy for me, there was something in her smile that seemed almost sad. "So, what do you think you're going to do?"

"I really love my job at the restaurant."

"I know you do."

"You know how much I think of Stephen. He's been nothing but good to me. But I came here for more than that. I hope that doesn't make me sound ungrateful, because I'm not. He and Mr. Boulud gave me a wonderful opportunity. In fact, besides Wenn, they're the only ones who gave me an opportunity. What they did for me means a great deal."

"It's not as if they didn't get something out of it, regardless of how brief your time might be with them. And your dreams never were to run a restaurant, Jennifer."

"They weren't. But if I leave them, I'll still feel guilty."

"You once told me that your job there is coveted."

"It is."

"So, don't you think they'll find a replacement sooner rather than later?"

I hadn't considered that. I knew they would. db Bistro was among the city's best restaurants. Of course they'd find someone soon, probably someone in-house. Or maybe someone from a competing restaurant. The pay was good and if you wanted to be in the restaurant business, having db Bistro on your resume would be very attractive.

"What do you owe them, really? You've done your job. You signed no contract to stay for any length of time. You've been professional and did everything they've asked of you. New offers come to people every day. Can they match five hundred grand? I'm thinking they can't. Anyone would jump at the opportunity you're being offered. Ask yourself this. Do you think Stephen would leave the restaurant for that kind of money."

"I have no idea."

"Really? Even if it advanced his career."

"He might."

"What do you think he earns?"

"I did some research on that before I went to them. For very good restaurants like db, a general manager can make as much as two hundred thousand."

"And Stephen wouldn't leave if he was offered an additional three hundred thousand to go somewhere else? Come on, Jennifer. Get real. This is business we're talking about. It's not personal."

"It feels personal."

"Well it shouldn't. But that's just you. Let me ask you the real question here. Is this something you'd like to explore with Wenn?"

I shrugged. "Working at Wenn would allow me two things. First, it's a dream job. I'll be able to become the true business junky that I am and assist the corporation with any number of ideas and strategies. That excites me. Alex will make that happen for me—and he'll listen to me. He takes me seriously. Second, I'll be able to be with Alex, which also is important to me. If we're going to make a go of this budding relationship, Lisa, I need to be able to spend time with him."

"I understand that. It's not going to work otherwise."

This time I saw a fleeting look of concern cross her face, and then it disappeared.

"What are you thinking about?" I asked.

"Nothing," she said.

"Come on, Lisa. Be honest with me. We know each other better than we know ourselves."

She looked up at me and her eyes filled with tears. "I think I'm going to lose you," she said.

"What are you talking about?"

"Jennifer, if you take this job—and I think you should—you'll be making half a million a year. I can't compete with that. You're not going to want to live here. You'll be out of here ASAP. I'm sorry if this sounds selfish, but I am going to miss you terribly when you go."

"Who says you're not coming with me?"

"Oh, Jennifer. Come on. You're on the verge of having a boyfriend now. You've gotten what you've fought for—a high-paying job doing exactly what you want. *If* you want it, and I know you do. I write about zombies, for Christ's sake. I'm getting by, but I am so far from your level now, it's not even funny."

"And when I was almost on my last dime, who was there for me? You were, time and again. During that period, I had the same concerns. I thought that if your new book hit, which I pray to God it does, you might leave me because I wouldn't be able to afford the lifestyle you'd want. And who could blame me? Who in their right mind would want to stay in this shithole any longer than they had to? I was worried sick that you'd hit the list again and want a better place. Maybe one of your own."

"You know I'd never do that to you."

"And you think I would do it to you? Seriously? What's the difference?"

That shut her up.

"We're a team," I said. "We've been one since we were kids. Do you really think I'd leave you behind because of any of this? I want you to enjoy this with me. I'm going to take the job, we are going to get out of this dump, and we are going to find a killer apartment where we can live together. Two sweet bedrooms. Two beautiful bathrooms. We can afford that now."

"I think you're being naïve."

"How?"

"Because he's going to want to be with you in your apartment. It's just natural. He's going to want to come over and spend time with you in *your* space, not ours. And when you fully give yourself to him, which will happen, he will want to spend the night with you *alone*, not with me there. Don't you see that?"

"You are my family," I said. "You have been since the fifth grade. Alex has a lovely space. When we want to be alone, we'll just go there. Occasionally, we'll all meet at our place and have dinner together. Oh, and by the way, he wants to cook for you."

She wrinkled her nose at me.

"That's what he said about an hour ago," I continued. "He wants to get to know you. He wants to cook dinner for both of us. He knows how important you are to me, and I think he instinctively knows that no one ever will come between us. If Alex and I want to be alone, big deal. He has a home for that. It's not rocket science. This is nothing for you to worry about, so please don't. In a hot second, I would give up him and this job before I ever gave you up. And don't think I'm joking. You mean everything to me. You know that."

"I don't want me and my zombies to hold you back."

"Your zombies are going to change your life after this next book. And the next book. And the next. Who are you kidding? You're already on your way."

"Jennifer, I might have hit the list once, but nothing is certain. I could fail the next time. It happens. In fact, it's been over four months since the last book came out, so it's unlikely that it *will* happen. Readers of ebooks want one book per month from writers, and that is nearly impossible for anyone to do, unless you're just writing shit or a novella. I'm an independent author. Yes, readers liked the first book a lot. Yes, the book was a best seller. But fans want the next book now, not next week. On my Facebook fan page, they're already grousing about when they can expect the next novel. And I mean *novel*. Not novella. Who can do that in a few months? I can't. That timeframe is unreasonable if they want the book to be good, which of course they do. I appreciate their enthusiasm, but let's get real. Writing a book takes time. But still they want it yesterday. And if they don't get it yesterday? It's on to the next author, who might be more prolific than me. I've seen it too many times. I've watched too many careers tank. Maybe I should cut this book into a series of shorts. Maybe that would appease them. Hell, I don't know. But I think that would be cheating them, so I won't. I also refuse to get in your way because of my own dilemma."

"You're not. Tomorrow, I'll agree to the job. I'll give db Bistro two weeks' notice. Then, we'll find a new apartment together. You and me. Something better than this joint. We deserve it. We deserve a real prize of an apartment, and we'll find it. But I won't do any of this without you. Do you hear me? None of this happens without you. I will refuse it all if you're not with me. You mean that much to me. OK?"

She leaned her head back against the sofa and sighed. "Jennifer—"

"OK?"

"I just don't think—"

"OK?"

"Fine," she said. "OK."

"You mean the world to me."

"I don't think I'm going to mean the world to Alex. I think I'll be in the way."

"He's not like that. He'll understand the situation."

"I love you, Jennifer. And I'm beyond happy for you. But I don't think you know what you're getting yourself into."

"What do you mean?"

"We'll see. And I sure as hell hope that I'm wrong."

CHAPTER EIGHT

The next night, when I gave my notice at db Bistro, Stephen hugged me and wished me well. "I knew we wouldn't be able to keep you long," he said. "Not someone like you. I just wish it had been longer, because I will miss you. But go out and live your dreams, Jennifer. We'll be fine, so stop looking so guilty. OK?"

I couldn't have asked for a better exit. The next morning, I told Alex that I would accept the job.

"Please tell me you're not joking."

"I'm not. But Lisa and I have to find a new place to live. It's not safe here. You know that. We each feel threatened by being here. I need you to be patient with me until we find a place. That's going to take a lot of work."

"It doesn't have to."

"Why's that?"

"Wenn has properties all over the city. If you'd like, I'll ask Blackwell to assist you. She knows them all, and she knows them well. She herself lives in one of our buildings. You could be neighbors."

"Very funny."

"She not that bad."

"I know she's not. Actually, she's grown on me. But I think another building might be best."

"Give it a shot—it's not like you're going to get a discount on rent, because I know you'd never have that. This is just an easy way to cut through the clutter. I'll have her call you and we'll nail this down fast so you and Lisa can get settled. Wenn provides moving assistance for all new employees, so you will be moved at no cost."

"Alex—"

"That's a fact, Jennifer. I'm not doing you a favor. Certainly you've heard of other corporations providing moving assistance. That's all this is."

Of course, I had. "All right."

"By going through us and because you now work for Wenn, this will be an easy transition by New York standards. No boards. No bullshit. And you know why?"

"Because you own Wenn?"

"Exactly. Expect a call from Blackwell. She'll find you a great place. And soon. Because I want to see you soon."

"Same here."

"I already miss you."

"I miss you, too."

"I'll have her set up appointments now. You'll hear from her within the hour. I'll give you all the space you need, because I know you'll find something quickly. Can I call you, at least?"

"I hope you do," I replied. "And text me whenever you want. I'm going to need that to get through these next two weeks."

"That's all I needed to hear. Talk soon. Text sooner. And have fun with Blackwell. She'll turn everything into a Broadway show."

When Blackwell called an hour later, just as Alex promised, she was her typical high-strung self. "So, now it's an apartment," she said.

"I guess it is."

"There are two of you?"

"There are?"

"What do you require?"

"A large space. Two bedrooms. Two baths. A terrace. A nice view. And a great kitchen. Anything else is a bonus."

"I can do all of that. What's your friend's name?"

"Lisa Ward."

"What does she do?"

"She writes about zombies."

"She writes about what?"

"The undead."

"Who does that?"

"Lisa."

"Well at last the undead are thin. Mostly skeletal, which is good. I could probably dress them for her."

"I'll let her know that."

"Please do. I'll see you in thirty minutes. Get ready, because it's going to be a whirlwind."

I decided to tease her. "Before you go, I have a confession."

"You have a what?"

"A confession."

"Save it for a priest."

"In this case, you are my priest."

"I'm plugging my ears."

"No, you're not."

"What is it, then?"

"Yesterday, I had a Big Mac. Large fries and a shake. At the end of the night, I had an entire bag of chips. It was fantastic."

"Don't you ever talk to me like that."

"I loved it. I thought of you the entire time I was gorging myself. I also think you would have loved it."

"Absolutely not. Salad, Jennifer. I told you. Salad. Roughage!"

"I might have gained a pound."

"You're going to be the end of me, Maine."

* * *

As usual, Blackwell got it right, and on the first try, which was no surprise to me at this point in our relationship because she always seemed to nail it on the first try. I think doing so was a source of pride for her—it's what drove her. But who knew—maybe she just got lucky, though I was beginning to seriously doubt that. She had skills I had yet to tap into. What mattered is that she always came through, even though she chastised me again for my "binging behavior" when she arrived by limousine to pick us up.

"I didn't binge," I told her when Lisa and I stepped into the car. "I gorged."

"On crap that will make you fat. How am I supposed to dress you for the next event? Tell me. How? I can barely fit that ass of yours into couture as it is."

"It hasn't been a problem so far."

"It will be if you keep that up."

She looked at Lisa and surmised her with a careful eye. "You're the one who writes about the undead?"

"I am," Lisa said.

"And you make a living doing so?"

"I do."

"The irony!"

Lisa laughed.

"What's wrong with writing about the living?" Blackwell asked.

"Everything."

"Everything?"

Lisa leaned toward her. "Don't you think the living disappoint?"

"Well," Blackwell said, straightening. "I can't exactly argue with *that*. Especially after recent divorce proceedings in my life. And I have to say, you are very pretty, Ward. Beautiful. And thin. Tiny. Probably a coveted size zero. Are you hearing me, Maine? Look at how tiny she is."

"I'm not listening to this."

"Ward, why would you let Jennifer go on a binge like that?"

"I don't control her, Ms. Blackwell."

"Who can? She's headstrong to the tenth degree. I can't keep her in a bottle to save my life—she always bursts out of it. I'm surprised she doesn't swing from vines."

"Excuse me?" I asked.

Blackwell ignored me and gave Lisa a questioning look. "Are you naturally blonde?"

"I am."

"Dip your head."

Lisa shot me an amused glance, and dipped her head.

"So you are. So rare. So Scandinavian. Are you Scandinavian? No? Just from Maine? I see. Well, regardless, I do have to admit that I admire your chic ensemble."

"I got it at Macys."

"You got it at what?"

"Macys. From the bargain bin. I think it was something like ninety percent off, with another five percent off if you had a coupon, which I did."

"Coupon?"

"That's right."

"Why am I suddenly faint? Can you see the gray edges closing in like I can? Do you see the demons? They're encroaching." She snapped her head at us. "Don't you ever say Macys, coupon or bargain in my presence again. Understood? Good. God! Do I need to teach you girls everything? Apparently. There are some things you just don't say around me or anyone else in this town. You'll send everyone whirling. Already I need something for my acid reflux. This is going to be a hellish day—I just know it."

"Sorry, Ms. Blackwell," I said.

"I've already told you to call me Barbara."

"I prefer Ms. Blackwell."

"Well," she said. "I mean, of course you do. I don't blame you. It does, after all, suit me."

* * *

Later, in the car, she said, "Where do you want to live?"

"Close to Wenn."

"That's the most sensible thing you've said today. So, Upper East Side?"

"That would be perfect."

"Where?"

"On Fifth?"

"Really, Maine. Fifth?"

"That's right."

"Well, who doesn't want to live on Fifth? But you're lucky. I've got the place. To die for. And with your new salary, you can afford it. You will blow kisses at me when you see it."

"We'll see."

"Oh, no, Maine. You'll be blowing me kisses straight up my ass. And you'll send me flowers for the privilege of doing so. You might even invite me to dinner, though I'd decline in an instant."

"Why?"

"Because you'd probably serve me something like McDonald's. Or you'd ply me with a pizza. Or some other assorted junk. You know I don't approve of eating. Ever."

"Oh, please."

"Oh, please, yourself. All one needs is black coffee, water, ice and a daily vitamin. Just you wait and see what I have in store for you two." She leaned toward the driver. "800 Fifth Avenue. STAT!"

"Do you think it has Park views?" Lisa asked me.

I shrugged. "Does it, Ms. Blackwell?"

"Does it what?"

"Have views of the Park."

She looked imperious as she lifted her chin and peered out the window to her right. "Park views. Do you really think I *wouldn't* give you Park views? Do you think so little of me? Do you think I lack vision? Common sense? A goddamned heart? Of course, you'll have Park views. And a hell of a lot more than that. Just you wait and see."

* * *

When we arrived at 800 Fifth, the driver pulled to the curb, and a valet came immediately to Blackwell's door to open it. The three of us got out and moved onto the busy sidewalk. Before we could enter the building, Blackwell turned each of us around so we were looking across the street.

"There's your Park."

She turned us around again so we were facing the building. "Your apartment is the penthouse. The one on the left. Can you see it from here? Probably not—too bright. But it's the thirty-fourth floor. Gorgeous."

"Penthouse?" Lisa said.

"Yes, that's right. Penthouse."

"I guess we really are movin' on up."

I smiled at her and broke into song. "To a de-luxe apartment in the ski-hi-hi."

"I don't know what that means," Blackwell said.

"Nothing," Lisa said.

"Sorry," I offered. "Just a bit of nostalgia."

"A bit of what?"

"Not important."

"Whatever. Let's go and have a look, shall we? It's only been on the market for two days. You are so in luck. If you like it, we get it now. As in right now. No dawdling. This apartment will go very quickly. By the end of tomorrow at the latest."

We were ushered into a massive lobby that was nicely furnished and had lots of natural light and a friendly looking man standing behind a desk to our right.

"Ms. Blackwell," he said.

Blackwell clicked over to him with purpose. "James, James, James. Sweet, James. So good to see you. Hellohoware? Are we the first?"

"I'm afraid not."

"Have any offers come in?"

"I wouldn't know. But by the looks of one couple, whom I saw leaving with their Realtor a few hours ago, I'm certain that one is coming."

"They had that look, didn't they?"

"They did."

"A happy little bounce in their step?"

"A definite bounce."

"And that awful, 'Can you fucking believe we finally found a place' look?"

"That was the look."

"*Merde*."

He gave her a key. "Perhaps if you move swiftly?"

"Of course. Please call management. Stall everything until we've seen it. No offers are to be accepted. That's coming from me and Mr. Wenn."

"Of course, Ms. Blackwell."

She looked at us. "Elevator. We're on a mission. Now."

*   *   *

When we arrived on the thirty-fourth floor, we took a right out of one of the elevators and went to the end of a long hallway where there was a door marked 34F. Blackwell wasted no time. She unlocked the door, swung it open, and said, "Let's do this."

We walked inside, and it was just glorious. A half-bath to our left with a closet next to it. Beautiful tiled floors. To the left was the living room, which had the most amazing views of the Park beyond a curtain of windows. On the other side of the foyer was a library or a dining room—however we wanted to use it. Probably a dining room. We followed Blackwell, who was pointing at this and at that, but all Lisa and I could do was shoot each other looks of disbelief. The space was massive. Two large bedrooms that had their own attached marble baths. A gourmet kitchen with granite counter tops and high-end, gleaming stainless steel appliances. Windows everywhere that flooded the space with light.

"I want it," I said. "Lisa?"

"It's amazing."

"Of course, it is," Blackwell said. "At least you two have the good taste to recognize good design in a flash."

"How much per month?"

"Ten thousand."

"Ten thousand?" Lisa said, looking crestfallen. "Oh."

"We'll take it," I said. "As in right now. Please make sure that all other offers are too late, and that this penthouse is ours."

Ms. Blackwell looked me coolly in the eye. "You wouldn't like to see anything else?"

"Why would I when you've already shown us perfection?"

"Sometimes I really like you, Maine."

"Sometimes it's mutual, Ms. Blackwell," I said. And when I said it, each of us tried to suppress a smile.

* * *

In the elevator, I texted Alex. "We've got our place. It's fantastic. Penthouse at 800 Fifth. More later. Miss you."

It was only a moment before he chimed in. "Very happy for you and Lisa. Great location. I wish I could pick you up from work tonight. Let's talk later. Miss you very, very much."

I smiled down at my phone and looked up to see the two women looking squarely back at me. "What?" I said.

"All of it's just so wrong," Blackwell said.

"What's so wrong?"

"That happy look on your face. I just went through a wretched divorce, and there you are smiling down at a smart phone with hooded eyes. It makes me want to vomit."

"Shall I share that with Alex?"

"You can spoon feed it to him. He knows what I went through. He knows how I am. And he loves me despite all of it."

"Actually, I do, too."

"Oh, Maine, puh-lease."

"You think you're tough, but you're actually a push-over."

"I am human Draino. I will eat through you if I need to."

"My zombies also can do that," Lisa said.

"Your what?"

"The undead peeps I write about?"

"Are you developing a new language? 'Undead peeps.' Where am I? What is that?"

The elevator started to slow.

"Anyway, I'm a force, Maine. You have no idea what you're dealing with." She fingered a few strands of her black bob away from her face and looked up at the elevator's dial as we approached the lobby. "Though I do appreciate our excursions. They're... What's that word I never use? Fun? No, too strong. Enjoyable? Maybe. I suppose I can live with that."

"I'm glad you can," I said. "How about if we sign the paperwork and have lunch? We need to get a burger in you."

"Maybe some mesclun," she acquiesced. "Drop of vinegar. I could probably do that. I actually have the perfect place in mind. And it's my treat since you two weren't entirely impossible today."

As we passed James in the lobby, she said to him, "It's a goner. Meet your new tenants, Jennifer Kent and Lisa Ward. They'll be moving in immediately. All the paperwork will be signed by day's end. Toodles, James. My sweet, sweet James. Toodles, toodles. Love, love, love. We're off for some roughage."

CHAPTER NINE

When I left work that night, it was odd and felt kind of lonely not to find Alex waiting outside for me. I stepped onto the sidewalk, saw his limousine idling at the curbside, and watched his driver pop out to open the rear door for me. Alex said he'd send a driver to make sure I got home safe, and, true to his promise, here was my ride home.

Or did I even want to go home?

A thought crossed my mind. I considered it as I stepped into the back of the limousine, and by the time the driver got back inside, I asked him to take me to Wenn.

"To Wenn?" the man asked.

"Please," I said. "I know Alex won't be there, but that's fine."

"Of course."

It was fine because Alex had given me a key to his apartment, which I had in my purse and which the driver likely knew about. And so we drove to Wenn. When we arrived, the driver opened my door and I asked him that when he did pick up Alex to please not mention that I was here.

"I want to surprise him," I said.

"Your secret's safe with me, Ms. Kent."

I thanked him, and stepped into the building. As I entered, the security guards at the front desk greeted me by name. I went over and asked them not to tell Alex that I was here when he arrived. They said they wouldn't.

"I appreciate that," I said.

"No problem, Ms. Kent."

"It's Jennifer," I said. "Please call me Jennifer."

"Of course, Ms. Kent."

I smiled at them, and walked behind their desk to Alex's private elevator. I slid my key into the slot, the doors opened, and I stepped in. The elevator lifted, and I sent a quick text to Lisa letting her know where I was. When I reached Alex's apartment, I pushed the button for the lobby before stepping out as the doors shut. I listened to the elevator plummet. Alex would expect the car to be waiting for him in the lobby when he slipped his key into the slot. Otherwise, he'd know that someone had used it, and he'd suspect that something was up. I wasn't having any of that.

I turned on lights, walked into his apartment, and texted him in the hallway. "I'm home," I wrote. "Any idea when you'll be home so we can talk? I'd like to hear your voice before I go to sleep."

When he chimed in, he wrote, "I should be just another hour. Don't go to sleep, OK? I also want to talk before we each turn in."

So, I had an hour. More than enough time.

I went into his kitchen, switched on the lights, and looked around for two martini glasses. I found them in one of the cupboards. I put them in the freezer, removed a chilled bottle of Grey Goose from the side of the freezer door, and searched for a glass pitcher of some sort. There was an elegant one with a silver handle in another cupboard. In it was a slender silver stirring stick. Vermouth was in the refrigerator, as were the olives I'd need later. Somewhere in here, I'd find the little silver spears he'd used for the olives in the martini he served me the other night.

When I finished making the pitcher of martinis, I put it in the freezer, looked around, and found some cocktail napkins and nuts in the pantry, and a silver bowl in another cupboard. I shook a heaping mound of nuts into the bowl, hurried it and the napkins into the living room, and placed both onto the table in front of the sofa.

That's that.

I sat on the sofa and looked at the beautiful New York skyline while thinking thoughts I shouldn't be thinking as I waited for him. To my surprise, after I'd been there for only forty minutes, he texted me. "I'm in the car now and on my way home. I hope you haven't gone to sleep. I really need to hear your voice, Jennifer."

I smiled at that, and wrote, "I'm up and waiting for you. How long?"

"Five minutes."

"I'll talk to you in ten."

Immediately, I was off the sofa. I poured two martinis into the chilled glasses, found the silver spears for the olives in the utensil drawer, and brought the drinks to the coffee table.

I sat down on the sofa, and felt a start. The lights were on. They were off when I got here. With a rush, I turned them off, felt my way back to the sofa, stretched out my legs along with my three-inch red pumps, and listened as the hum of the elevator lurched into motion.

My heart quickened as he neared me. I was wearing a short, off-white, silk skirt, and a silk blouse opened at the neck that was the same color as my shoes. No jewelry. My hair was down, just as he liked it. A hint of my cleavage showed. I tried like hell to adjust myself into a position so I would look like a feast to him, but I had no idea what I was doing, so I just made the effort to look like something out of one of Lisa's fashion magazine ads. I was all angles, a pair of long legs, a bust of boobs, and a mane of hair. I felt ridiculous.

I am so over my head when it comes to these sorts of things. What am I doing? I look like a total amateur. This isn't coquettish. This is a travesty.

But at least I'd tried.

I took a quick sip of my martini to calm my nerves, but a sip hardly was enough to do the job. Still, the drink was icy cold and it tasted good, which is what mattered most to me. Just a hint of vermouth, and the brine of the olives. I wanted him to have a proper drink when he got home. Something to soothe his nerves.

When the elevator doors slid open and I heard his initial footfalls into the penthouse, I held my breath and sat completely still as lights in the foyer flashed on. I heard him sigh. I didn't know where he'd gone tonight—he didn't mention it to me and I forgot to ask. But he had said this event would be longer than the others, and it was. I could only imagine its importance. I wondered if he was able to keep the wolves at bay and get some business done. Soon, once I came on as a consultant, that wouldn't be an issue for him any longer.

I could hear him move toward the living room. I bit my bottom lip and waited for him to step inside. When he did, he flipped on the lights. And then he froze when he saw me.

For a moment, we just looked at each other. There was shock on his face, but it was instantly replaced by a grin.

"What are you doing here?"

"I wanted to see you. I hope it's OK."

"Of course it's OK. I gave you a key for this very reason. I thought I wasn't going to see you tonight. I can't tell you how happy this makes me."

"I wanted to surprise you, Mr. Wenn."

"Well, you did, Ms. Kent. In the best way."

He wasted no time coming over to me. I stood and fell into his embrace, which was warmer than usual. The way he held me was different—it almost felt as if he was relieved. He kept his head on my shoulder for a moment longer than usual, and he breathed in my scent. I felt his body relax against mine. After a moment, I pulled back and kissed him.

"I can't imagine a better surprise," he said.

"I can't imagine a better way to end the day."

His eyes were inflamed by the fact that I was here with him. "You look sexy as hell," he said in a low voice.

"Is that how you talk to all of your new employees?"

"Just one."

"And by the way, I should return the compliment. But then, you know that whenever I see you in a tux, I just sort of turn into a puddle on the floor...."

"One day, we'll have to psychoanalyze that."

"You've said that before, but why bother? Just keep wearing them, and I'll be a happy woman. I obviously have some sort of suit fetish when it comes to you. Doesn't matter which one you wear. Unless, of course, down the road, it's you in your birthday suit. Who knows? That might be my favorite of all."

"Jennifer—"

Even I blushed at my comment. *Slow down, girl.* I deflected. "I made you a martini."

He looked down at the coffee table, and saw the two drinks, the napkins and the nuts.

"You came here and did all of this for me?"

"It wasn't exactly difficult. And it isn't that much. I found what I could in the kitchen. I hope you don't mind."

There was a tenderness in his voice when he said, "That kitchen is yours as well as mine. It's the thought behind what you did that matters. I know you've been on your feet all night, and still you came here to do this. I'm grateful."

I touched his face and kissed him again. Only this time, there was no holding him back. He was strong— stronger than he looked, which was saying something, because he was nothing if not built. He swept me into his arms, pulled me in as if we were one, and kissed my lips, my neck, and the concave of my throat with a fierceness that I responded to. I felt my nipples stiffened with arousal when he leaned into me. Apparently, I wasn't the only one who was aroused. The thought of him pressed against my thigh like that sent me over the edge with desire. I wanted him so much, but it needed to wait. He was right. This had to build until we could no longer stand it.

But that didn't mean we couldn't have fun along the way.

Tonight, even if it was only for an hour or so, we were going to cuddle on the sofa in each other's arms, have our martinis, enjoy each other, talk about our days, and then I'd be on my way. I knew he needed to get up early. I didn't want him exhausted when he woke.

But I wasn't going to let him off that easily.

I sat on the sofa and extended a leg. "Would you mind removing my shoe, Mr. Wenn?"

His eyes flicked up to meet mine, and then he crouched down and unbuckled it with ease. He massaged my foot before I extended my other one. "And this?"

"My pleasure, Ms. Kent."

He released my foot from it. Then, unexpectedly, he started to kiss each of my toes, then he popped my little toe into his mouth and swung his tongue around it as he gently sucked it. The sensation was undeniably erotic. I pressed back against the sofa and let him do whatever he wanted to do to me. As he worshiped my feet with his mouth, his right hand roamed up my right thigh until it disappeared beneath the fabric of my skirt. His hand went deeper, he tugged at my panties, and his finger slipped just beneath them. Then, looking at me, I knew he'd felt my wetness. He pulled back and smoothed his hand back down the length of my leg to my foot.

I was almost breathless when I said, "Take off your shirt."

"What if I don't want to?"

"Then you'll be waiting for this much longer than you planned. Stand up and take off your shirt."

"Who's in control now?" he asked as he stood.

"We both are. We're equals here."

"Somebody has to be in charge."

"Did you just arrive from the fifties? I may be a virgin, but I know what I want. In fact, because I've waited this long, I probably know more about what I want than most women."

"Good point." He paused. "I may need help with my jacket," he said.

"I'd rather watch."

"But if you helped, I could get out of it quicker."

"I'm in no hurry. And you're the one who sent that photo of yourself. I can't get it out of my head. It's cruel what you did to me. It's my right to see you shirtless in person."

"What about that photo you sent of yourself? That wasn't cruel?"

"That was payback."

He had an amused look on his face when he shrugged off this jacket. He tossed it onto a chair, released his cuff links, put them on the table, and said, "Are you sure about this?"

"I want to see you."

And with that, slowly—too slowly for my taste—he pulled off his tie, tossed it aside, unbuttoned his shirt and removed it. He let it drop to the floor and stood bare-chested in front of me. I thought he looked masculine, muscular and magnificent. My gaze roamed over his broad chest, his taut nipples, and his ripped torso. What I saw was enough to linger over. I just soaked it in.

"Happy?" he asked.

"Almost."

"What would make you happier?"

"This."

Before he could react, I stood and cupped my hands over his chest. His skin was smooth and his chest was lightly hairy. I could feel his heart begin to pound against my hands, and then I lowered my head, put my mouth over one of his nipples, and nipped and tugged on it with my teeth until he couldn't bear it any longer. He reached behind me and pulled me away from him by the back of my hair with just enough force that it was a little rough, which I decided I rather liked because I felt safe with him.

"You're in a mood," he said.

"Don't read too much into it."

He let go of my hair. "Take off your shirt," he said.

"No."

"It's a fair request."

"Why don't you have a sip of your martini instead?"

"Maybe I will when you take off your shirt."

I would never bare my breasts to him—at least not yet—but really, if I did take off my shirt, I wouldn't be baring anything more than if I were in a bikini. That seemed safe enough, not to mention sexy—and I was nothing if not turned on right now.

"How much do you want it?" I asked.

His voice was almost a growl when he said, "I think you know much I want it."

"That doesn't answer my question, Alex."

"I want it as much as I want you. I want it because I deserve to see you, just as you've seen me. Now, please, take off your shirt."

I sat him down on the sofa, handed him his martini, and tossed my hair over my head when I stood up. "You think you can handle it?"

He made a low noise in his throat as he looked up at me.

I nodded at his cocktail. "Drink up, stud. You're going to need it."

Whatever awkwardness I'd felt earlier when I tried to position myself on the sofa was gone. I knew it was in his nature to be in control, but he was allowing me to be in control, which was disarming because I'd never done anything like this before. For whatever reason, I still wanted the control. I liked the control. I liked the effect it had on him, and also on me. In a strange way, all of this felt natural to me. He was bringing out a side of me that I didn't recognize, but that I wanted to explore.

I unbuttoned the top of my shirt to reveal the lacy red bra I wore beneath. He kept his eyes on me the entire time, only sipping his drink once as I completed the task. I untucked the shirt from my skirt and stood before him with my midsection bared to him. "Do you want to take it off me, Mr. Wenn? Or are you just going to sit there and just stare at me?"

"I could look at you all day."

"That doesn't answer my question."

"If you need assistance—"

"Assistance would be nice."

When he stood, I could see his arousal in his pants. It looked impossibly large to me, which at once thrilled me and terrified me, particularly when he came up behind me and pressed it against my ass. I hadn't seen that part of him yet, but I was no fool. Alex obviously was well endowed.

How am I ever going to take that thing?

He pressed his hands against my flat stomach and held me for a moment, the stubble on his chin igniting my body as he kissed my neck and continued to slowly grind into me.

"Do you like that?" he asked.

I tried to keep my voice even, but it took an effort. "I thought you were here to help me take off my shirt?"

He smoothed his hands up my body, stopped to caress my breasts, which felt unusually full and heavy to me, and then nibbled very lightly on my ear. I could feel his hot breath against my skin when he told me how beautiful I was. I wanted to turn to him and kiss him, but I didn't. I wanted it like this. I wanted to deprive myself, and in the end, I also wanted to deprive him. This is how it was going to build, even if it was becoming more and more difficult to deny what I was feeling. The wetness between my legs only became more pronounced as he pressed his bulge squarely between the cleft in my buttocks where he rubbed it up and down. He was in no hurry to remove my shirt, so much so that I wondered who was in control now. Him or me?

Me.

I turned to him and kissed him on the cheek. "That was nice," I said. "But you've lost your chance."

He looked confused as I started to button up my shirt.

"What are you doing?"

"Getting dressed."

"But you said I could remove your shirt."

"You took too long."

Gently, he took my hands in his own and I could tell by the fire in his eyes that this wasn't ending now. Not that I wanted it to. "Hold your hands behind your back, Jennifer."

I did as I was told, and he unbuttoned the two buttons I'd fastened before he stopped me. When he removed my shirt, he tossed it behind me onto the sofa and took a step back to admire me. Or at least that's what it felt like. I'd never seen such passion on his face.

"Shouldn't we go to my bedroom?" he asked.

"I don't think that should happen at all. Not yet. Too soon."

"You didn't come here just for a martini, Jennifer."

"True. I came here to see you."

"Without a shirt on?"

"The idea might have crossed my mind."

"I told you once that there are things I can do to you without barely touching you. Do you remember that?"

I felt my heart quicken. How much more of this could I take and still hold back from being with him? "I remember."

"I can do that now if you'd like."

"I think we should wait."

"Can I ask you a personal question?"

"We're practically naked, Alex. What's stopping you?"

He smiled at that, and then he became serious. Almost hesitant. "You don't have to answer this, but I'm curious. Have you ever had an orgasm?"

I didn't flinch. "No," I said. "I haven't."

He furrowed his brow. "You've never masturbated?"

"Haven't done that, either."

This seemed to perplex him. "Why?"

"Because a long time ago, I told myself that I would wait for the right man. A whole host of reasons have held me back, but much of it comes down to the way my father treated my mother and me. I wanted more than that. I knew I deserved more than that." I shrugged. "I know I have trust issues because of my father. So, I've waited and will continue to wait until I know that I can fully trust the right man, whomever he might be."

"Are you working out trust issues with me?"

"Alex, I work them out with anyone who comes to mean something to me. So, yes, I am, but it's not just you. It's anyone who enters my life. Please understand that it's not personal. But I will say this. My emotions are skating to the edge of the cliff with you. I've never put my trust in someone the way I've put it in you. Not even with Lisa, because this is intimate in ways that she and I will never will be intimate. This is a whole new level for me."

"I'm glad you're trying."

"I have to. At some point, I need to take a chance and trust. I feel my best bet is with you."

His face was tense during the exchange, but lives aren't scripted, and conversations sometimes don't go down the wanted path. There was a silence between us now that I wanted to get past. I cocked my head at him. "I'm not perfect," I said.

"To me, you are."

He took a breath as if to settle his nerves. A moment ago, we were slammed against the hot asphalt of raw emotion, but then the trust issue thing came up and threw water on all of it. But I wasn't going to lie to him. I came into this relationship with baggage, just as I sensed that he did because of the death of his wife. In some ways, both of us were fully capable, adjusted human beings. In other ways, we were broken by past events.

"Can I ask you another question?" he asked.

"You can ask me a dozen questions."

"Do you think I'm the right man?"

"You've done things to me that no man has ever been allowed to do."

"Have you enjoyed them?"

"You know I have."

"Then nothing more is happening tonight. Your first time will be special. It will be everything you've wanted it to be. If it's with me, I'll make certain of that. But if we continued doing what we were doing a moment ago, I could go too far and bring you to climax. You deserve better."

"You sound awfully sure of yourself."

"That's because I am. I could whisper in your ear and make you come right now. No touching, nothing. Just my voice. And it would happen, Jennifer. You would come."

The thought of it almost made me want to do it.

"Here," he said, brushing past me to the sofa where my shirt was laying. "Put this back on before you drive me crazier than you already have." He stood behind me and held out the shirt so I could put my arms through the sleeves. When I had, he stepped in front of me and kissed me on the mouth while he buttoned my shirt. Then the kiss deepened, and soon he was pressing against me again. I closed my eyes and felt myself quiver before he finally broke away.

"Sorry," he said.

"What for?"

He didn't respond. Instead, he finished buttoning my shirt.

"May I do the same for you?" I asked.

"You can do whatever you want."

I picked up his shirt from the floor, but then stopped. "You probably don't want to put this back on. It's stiff with starch and it won't be very comfortable."

He went over to the sofa and leaned back against it. "I don't need a shirt." He patted the cushion next to him and said, "Come and sit with me. Let's talk about the day."

I went over and sat next to him. We talked about the penthouse on Fifth, and he told me about the party he had been to earlier. Eventually, my head was resting on his stomach, my hand was just above his groin, and after a while, we lapsed into silence. He stroked my hair, and I smoothed my hand over his velvety skin. It was a comfortable silence. It was the best kind of silence. It was the sort of silence that underscored the power of our bond and how unnecessary words could be between two people. Because even in this silence, we were talking to each other. Energy passed between us, and the evening took a different shape. I listened to the steady rhythm of his heart, I held him closer to me, and then I closed my eyes and fell asleep.

CHAPTER TEN

When I woke the next morning, it was with a start, and for a moment, I was discombobulated.

There was a thin blanket over me. My head was resting on a pillow. I wasn't sure where I was, but as I sat up, it came flooding back to me. Last night, when I was resting my head on Alex's stomach, I must have dozed off. Still, I had to wonder. I was a light sleeper and had been since I was a child. It was a protective measure against my father, who would storm into my room drunk at any hour of the night shouting at me, punching me and threatening me with my life for no reason other than to terrorize me. How had Alex got up without waking me? Had I been that tired?

Or was I just that comfortable with him?

I looked around for him, and when I did, I saw a glass of orange juice on the coffee table in front of me. My mouth was dry so I sipped it. It was tart and freshly squeezed.

Then, from the kitchen, Alex spoke. "Someone's up."

"That would be me," I said.

"Come and have breakfast," he said. "It's still very early. Not even six yet. We've got plenty of time together before I have to jump into the shower and get ready for the day."

I took my glass of juice and went into the kitchen, unprepared to find Alex shirtless and in just a pair of pale blue boxer shorts. The sight was disarming, not that I was going to ask him to do anything about it. He looked hot. He was sitting at the bar with the *Times* in front of him. I went over to him, put my arms around his broad shoulders, then dropped them around his tight waist, and held him before I sat next to him. I kissed him on his stubbly cheek, then on his lips.

"Coffee?" he asked.

"That would be nice."

He stood. "You got it."

"How long have you been up?" I asked, watching him walk away from me. He had a deep cleft in his back, which I thought was beyond sexy. And then there was his butt, which was about as perfect as they came.

And people talk about my ass. They should see his.

"Just about an hour or so."

"Do you always get up early?"

"I do, but I have a process. I need coffee, quiet, the paper, silence. After the first cup or two, I'm ready to go."

"Are you my twin?"

"You're the same way?"

"You have no idea."

"Then I'll be quiet and make coffee."

I put my elbows on the bar and put my chin in my hands as I watched him use a coffee press. Was that another trick he learned from his childhood cook, Michelle? Not many knew how to do it right, but I did, and from watching him, it looked as if did he. When he was finished, he added the exact amount of cream and sugar that I liked. He must have watched me prepare my own coffee two mornings ago when he made eggs for me.

This man doesn't miss a trick.

The coffee and its heady aroma were enough to clear my head. For breakfast, we had chilled pineapple chunks to start, which were delicious, then the lightest of scrambled eggs served with a fresh croissant that was warm and buttered. Neither of us talked until my second cup of coffee arrived and the plates were carefully removed so as not to make too much noise. He was nothing if not a gentleman.

"Satisfied?" he finally asked.

"Completely," I said. "You're such a good cook."

"It's all Michelle."

"She was your escape when you were a child?"

I saw a brooding look come over his face, but he masked it. "She was. I think I told you that."

Which meant that's as far as he was going to go.

"Look," he said. "You're just waking up. Why trouble you with my past now?"

That was mysterious. I knew from Blackwell that he hadn't been close to his mother, but never once had she mentioned his father. Alex had, though. When we first met at the interview, he suggested that he never wanted to take over Wenn, but he had because his father wrote it into his will. Then, the other day, he mentioned how Michelle also kept him clear of his father. So, the family didn't get along. I wondered why? And then it occurred to me that we had more in common than I realized, especially if I considered his issues with his father. I respected boundaries, so I let it pass. When he wanted to talk to me about it, he would. I certainly wasn't going to press. Of all people, I knew what it was like to not want to discuss your private life or your past.

I moved forward. "Sorry I fell asleep on you. Actually, literally on top of you."

"I'm not. Because of that, I get to have you here this morning."

"I have to say that your abs, as solid as they are, made for a nice place to lay my head last night."

"You don't say?"

"I do say."

I could tell that made him happy because he winked at me.

"What does your day look like?"

"The same. Back-to-back meetings, then an event tonight. But I'll be able to pick you up at the restaurant this time."

"I'd like that. I know this sounds silly, but the reason I came here last night is because I felt lonely when you weren't there to meet me after work last night. I came here on impulse. I wanted to see you. I just didn't think I'd be spending the night with you."

When I said that, Lisa entered my thoughts. "Lisa," I said.

"I've already talked with her. She knows you're here and that you're safe. Even though I wanted to carry you to one of my guest rooms, she suggested I leave you on the couch so you could get some sleep. I was climbing into my own bed when I called her. I knew you'd be concerned that you hadn't talked to her last night, so I took care of it for you after I tucked you in."

"Thank you—I appreciate that. Did she say anything?"

"Just that she's excited about the new apartment, and that she's eager for us to meet. I said that soon, we three could have dinner here. She was way up for that."

"Lisa is as tiny as they come, but when it comes to good food, there's no stopping her. Dinner with the three of us would be fantastic. I love her."

"She was a pip on the phone."

"She's wonderful. I'm so grateful for her. We've had a rough few months together."

"Things are better now."

"They are. Because of you."

"No, not because of me. You earned your job with db, Jennifer. They were lucky to have you. When you leave and assume your second job at Wenn, you'll see that you also earned that job. Your schedule will be hectic. You'll be with me night and day."

"And that's a bad thing?"

"We'll have our moments. We'll spar, it will get heated, and both of us will get pissed off at each other at some point along the way, but that's good. In fact, it's necessary. If we're considering a deal, we need to look at every possible angle and riff off each other to make sure it's the right deal to propose to the board. Just please don't think I gave you something because it's what you proposed. That's not how I work. It's not good business. You already proved yourself with Stavros. Because of you, Wenn will make a fortune off that deal. But I'll warn you. When it comes to the board, they'll be expecting you to bring it time and again. They'll expect you to pull another Stavros Shipping out of your hat. That's why we'll work closely together. Before I present anything to them, you and I will have fully fleshed out the pros and cons of any potential deal. We'll have each other's backs. We'll go to events at night, we'll mingle, we'll listen to what people are saying and how Wenn might be a part of the conversation. From that alone, we'll strike deals. And then we'll come here, have a drink, and we can settle into each other for a few hours."

"I worry about Lisa."

"What about?"

"I'll be with you a lot. She'll be alone a lot. We've always been together. I wish I could find someone for her."

"Is she looking?"

"She says she isn't, but I know better. Of course she'd like to be in a loving relationship. Not too long ago, her ex burned her, so she's pouring everything she has into her novels. It's her escape. Don't think she writes about the undead by chance. I think she sees her two former boyfriends among that bunch. But it would be terrific if she could meet someone who is on par with her. She's extremely bright and kind, and very, very pretty. But it's tough to meet a good man regardless of where you live. Most just want a hook-up, which neither Lisa nor I want. We are the antithesis of most young women in Manhattan. No bars. No fooling around. Nothing like that. We came from Maine focused to make it, and we didn't do so lightly. Still, I'd love to see her with a sweet guy who's ready to settle down."

"I have a few friends who are ready for that."

"Are they as hot as you? And as likable, as thoughtful, as sexy, and as interesting?"

"That's a tall order, ma'am."

I laughed.

"But they're all nice guys," he said. "As for the hotness factor, I can't give an opinion on that. I don't look at them that way—they're my buddies. But I've seen women go nuts over them. And not because they're wealthy, because no one knows that about them. So, when it comes to sex appeal, they've obviously got something going on. I will say that one of my good friends, Michael, seems to be a particular catch, but at this point in his life, he wants what I want. An equal. A good partner. A best friend. Not just a quick lay. He's old enough now that he wants to settle down. I've been waiting years for that to happen for me, and I think it has. So, maybe we invite Michael to have dinner with Lisa and us?"

"I'll talk to Lisa about it."

"You're a good girlfriend."

I didn't know how he meant that. "To her?"

"Yes, to her. And to me. I know to you that I'm just your companion, but for me, it's different. I think of you as my girlfriend. I want you as my girlfriend. It's my hope that one day, I can tell everyone that you're my girlfriend. When you let me know that I can, that will be one of the happiest days of my life."

And what was I supposed to say to that?

CHAPTER ELEVEN

My last two weeks at db passed more quickly than I anticipated. The restaurant was busy, which made the days go by quickly. I spent my free time in the mornings and afternoons with my nose buried in the *Journal* and in the *Times* to be prepared for what was coming next in my position with Wenn. Already I had some ideas.

I spent what time I could with Alex, which generally meant going to his apartment when my shift was over, and each of us talking about our day over a glass of wine or a martini.

The sexual tension was growing between us, which made for some interesting late evenings, though I hadn't stayed the night again. When I did that again, it would be for a very good reason.

On my last day of work, after the restaurant closed and my final shift ended, the staff came out with a cake for me, with Stephen holding it in front of him and leading the charge.

The cake, a lovely dark chocolate confection, was lit with a single candle, and everyone, including the chefs, was there to say their farewells to me.

Even though I'd only been there a short time, I couldn't help tearing up at the sight of that cake and the kindness behind it. In such a short period, we'd become a team. I didn't realize I'd feel so emotional at the finality of the situation, but I was. I was grateful to have had such a wonderful job, regardless of how brief it lasted. This place pulled me out of the financial fire and allowed me to stay in New York. I felt indebted to it.

Stephen placed the cake on a table.

"Please don't make me cry," I said.

"I can't promise you that, since you're already practically doing so. But I hope you'll promise us one thing."

"What's that?"

"That you'll come back and visit us."

"Did you think I wouldn't?" I said, hugging him. "I'll be back sooner than you think. Hell, I might even work a shift!"

* * *

When I left the restaurant, Alex was waiting outside for me. He was leaning against his limousine, and on his face was a trace of concern. I kissed him quickly on the lips before I slipped inside, and he followed after me.

"You're upset," he said.

"I'll be fine. I'm just a little sad, I guess. They were wonderful to me a moment ago. They brought out a cake." I wiped my eyes and took a deep breath. "This is silly," I said. "I'm sorry."

"Why do you feel the need to apologize? I'm sure that was difficult." He grabbed my hand and held it in his lap. "Tomorrow is a new day. Tomorrow, you're an employee at Wenn. At this point, most of your belongings are in your new apartment. I've talked with Lisa, who has overseen much of the move, and she said that there are just a few things left. Those will be taken care of in the morning and you both will be in your new digs by the afternoon."

"Thank you."

"It's my pleasure." He was quiet for a moment, and then said, "You know what?"

I turned to him, my eyes still bright with emotion. "What?"

"I haven't had a vacation in over four years."

His wife died four years ago. Blackwell told me that since then, all he did was work. I wondered where he was going with this, but said nothing so he could talk.

"I haven't visited the family compound in Maine since I was a teen. I want to take a week off with you and go there. I deserve it. You deserve it. The board has approved of it. I've sent members of my staff there to prepare it for us. They've been there this past week freshening it up. When they leave, and if you agree to come with me, it will just be us. No business. No city. Just us. It's been so long since I've been there that I hardly remember what the place looks like. But I need to remember. I need to live a little bit again. If you're willing, I'd like to spend a week there with you. I want to go to lobster shacks, I want to do some shopping, and mostly, I just want it to be with you with no intrusions. The board has been advised of that. Zero communication, unless it's an absolute emergency. Then, we'll come back to Manhattan, and start in with work. Are you up for that? Will you come with me?"

So, here it was—the next level. If I went with him, there was no question what would happen between us. But it was time. Who knew when it would happen when we got there, but it would happen. He'd take me. It was time to put my full trust in him. And I was eager to do so.

"I know what you're thinking," he said. "It doesn't have to be that."

Yes, it does. "When would we fly out?"

"Tomorrow at nine. We'll take one of the corporate jets straight into Bar Harbor. With car time, we should be there in less than two hours."

"Tomorrow morning? But I'll need time to pack."

"Lisa helped me out there. She gave me all of your measurements. Blackwell also helped to that end. I've had a complete wardrobe sent to the house for you. All of your favorite toiletries are waiting for you. Everything you need. And if you find that you need anything else, we'll just go to Ellsworth and buy it."

"How long has Lisa known about this?"

"A week."

"She never said a word to me about it."

"Your friend can keep a secret."

"Apparently."

"She's wonderful. I see why you're so close. So, you'll come?"

"Of course I will." I held him closer to me, but this time it was different. This time I truly felt him, and it felt right. I felt connected to him in ways that I hadn't before. It was foreign territory for me, but it wasn't unwelcome. I felt safe with him. I wanted to tell him that I was going because I *was* his girlfriend, not his companion. But for whatever reason I couldn't define, the words wouldn't come. Instead, I said, "I'm so grateful for you, Alex."

"You don't know what that means to me," he said.

CHAPTER TWELVE

It was close to noon the next day when we arrived at his home on the Point. It was located in a stunning location, right along the shoreline and overlooking the mountains, with Bar Harbor in the distance. It was completely private. Tall pines and trees that were just starting to turn color due to the oncoming fall surrounded it.

The air was so fresh that I just soaked it in when I stepped out of the car. That was one of the things I missed about Maine. You could breathe the air. After spending a mostly suffocating summer in the city, the salty ocean air was wonderful, as were the cool breeze and the sound of the waves lapping against the shore.

"Let me show you inside," he said.

The house was large, but not ridiculously so. It looked freshly painted to me, and in fact, I had a feeling it was. Surrounding it were beds of flowers that appeared newly planted. The windows gleamed as if they'd just been washed. He had told me he'd had people there to freshen up the place, but that was an understatement. It was clear to me that the house had been scrubbed and polished for this visit.

"This is a weird feeling," he said as he stuck his key into the lock and opened the door. "I honestly can't remember when I was here last. At least fifteen years ago, if not more."

I followed him inside and could smell a hint of new paint. The hardwood floors were polished and waxed—they caught the sun coming through the windows and tossed it back. We entered into the kitchen, which had all new stainless steel appliances, likely because the old ones needed to be replaced if it had been fifteen years since anyone had been there. As we walked from room to room, I took in the bright white trim and the subtle, bluish-gray walls, and then the magnificent views themselves.

He gave me the full tour, along with little vignettes as memories surfaced. "This was my father's library," he said, sticking his head briefly into the room before turning away from it. "And over here is where mother would read."

"They didn't read together?"

"They didn't do much together."

I decided not to probe, and kept pace behind him. We viewed guest bedrooms, a stunning living room with full views of the ocean, bathrooms, and finally the master bedroom, which was on the second level, just above the living room, and which shared its panoramic views. Here, the paint on the walls was a soft, muted shade of green, and the king-sized bed was obviously new, as were the beds in the rest of the house. I watched him cross to a closed door, and he opened it for me. Inside was the wardrobe he promised. "This is your room," he said. "I hope you find the clothes suitable."

"This used to be your parents' bedroom?"

He shook his head. "My mother took this room. My father took one of the guest bedrooms. I had one of the other ones."

"They didn't sleep together?"

"They couldn't stand each other, Jennifer. Their marriage was a sham. It was hostile. But let's not talk about that now. Later. First let's walk down by the shore."

He obviously was on his way to opening up little by little to me. Fair enough. I knew what it was like to be pressed on unpleasant matters when it came to family, so I said nothing and just chose to listen. Whatever he hadn't shared with me in the past would come out in time, probably during the ensuing week, and I wanted him to feel comfortable when and if he did so.

"Where will you be sleeping?" I asked.

"Just around the corner. In the room we saw before coming here. Are you OK with that? I could move to one of the other rooms down the hall if you'd like."

"No," I said. "I think you should take this room."

He grinned at me. "Not on your life. When you wake in the morning, the first thing I want you to see is that." He pointed to the window and beyond it to the wide expanse of ocean. It was lovely, but I thought he also should see it when he woke.

And really, Alex, the first thing I'd like to see when I wake is you. So, let's see how the day goes....

The shore was a mix of rocks, pebbles and what looked like gravel. Maine had only a few sand beaches; otherwise, much of the oceanfront was raw and rough to its core, not unlike many of the natives who lived there.

The tide was out, leaving clumps of seaweed in its wake, and the sun was brilliant. Alex reached out for my hand and we started to walk along the water, our shoulders nearly touching. I released my hand from his and wrapped it around the low of his back so he was closer to me. He wore jeans, a white T-shirt, and sandals. I was in yellow shorts, a white tank top, and also a pair of sandals. The wind was strong enough to whip my hair around my face, and, even though I knew I'd look like a hot mess when we got inside, I didn't care. This felt like heaven to me.

"Look," I said. "Just ahead of you on that large rock. A starfish."

"I remember seeing them when I was a boy."

We went over and knelt beside it. It was small and orange, with bluish bumps on its back. I carefully stroked it, admired it for a moment, and then left it alone. In the well of water surrounding the rock, I also noticed a tiny crab that danced away from me when I tried to touch it. It raised its claws in defiance, regardless of the fact that my hand dwarfed it. I didn't want to frighten it—not that it looked as if it could be frightened—so I also left it alone.

"It's magic here," he said. "Especially now. When I was a kid, it scared the hell out of me when I was told we were coming to Maine."

"Why?"

"Because this never was a happy place. After a certain point in their relationship, my parents shouldn't have been together. Here, they had to deal with their feelings for each other because there was nowhere else to go. There was no place to hide, as there was in Manhattan where they could each do their own thing whenever they wanted to. So, they fought constantly here. I remember wishing as a boy that they'd just divorce each other, but as I grew older, it became clear that my mother never would grant my father the divorce he wanted. She wanted all that came with the Wenn name. Of course, she would have kept the name regardless of a divorce, but she knew that my father would have crushed her socially, and that all she'd be left with was a portion of his money. So they stuck it out for all the wrong reasons. That's why being in a good relationship is important to me. I don't ever want what they had. I had a chance once with Diana, but then she was taken from me." He looked at me while we walked. "I didn't think I'd

Christina Ross

have that chance again. Now, four years later, here you are. I'm so happy that you're here."

"You've never shared any of this with me. I know that was difficult. It's still hard for me to talk about my own parents. It can be painful remembering what I'd rather not relive, but I think it's important for you to know what I came from. It will help you understand why I am who I am. Thanks for trusting me."

"You're way ahead of me in terms of addressing your past with your parents. At least you can talk about it. For me, it's almost impossible, but you're here now, and it's time for you to get to know more about me and where I came from. Then you can decide for yourself if you still want to be with me. You once said to me that you weren't perfect. Well, I'm far from perfect, Jennifer. I've got my own demons to wrestle with."

"Which ones?"

"Too many to count."

I stopped him. "Whatever your parents did to each other is no reflection on you, Alex. Same goes for my father. And for my mother's complete lack of intervention. What they did to me is on them, not me. Did my father's ranting, drunken idiocy affect me? Of course it did. Still does. Feel free to share whatever you want with me, but you don't have to share what you don't want to. I trust you enough to know that I can talk to you without being judged. I hope you'll come to feel the same with me."

"I already do," he said. "That's one of the reasons we're here."

CHAPTER THIRTEEN

For dinner, it was lobster rolls and fries. We drove into town and I bought us two rolls each at a local restaurant before Alex had time to pull out his wallet. Then, we brought them back in large Styrofoam containers to the house.

When Alex opened the refrigerator, I noticed that someone had stocked it to the nines. He did a little searching and then removed a bottle of champagne. I recognized it on sight from my time at db Bistro. The bright orange label gave it away. Veuve Clicquot. Stephen gave me a taste of it once. I told him I was only used to the cheapest of champagnes.

"Cheap is what I can afford," I said.

"You'll work harder after sipping this," Stephen had replied.

As usual, Stephen was right. The champagne was bright and intoxicating.

"We're really roughing it now," I said to Alex.

"Indeed, we are."

He popped open the bottle, found two antique champagne glasses in one of the cupboards, and poured. From the bottom of the glass' hollow stem, bubbles swirled to the top and popped.

"To Maine," he said, holding up his glass.

"To Maine," I agreed. "And to lobster. Look how fat these rolls are. I'm salivating. If she knew what I was eating, Blackwell would have my ass."

"She'd like to have your ass."

"Just her?"

"I think you know better."

We touched glasses, sipped, and dug in.

"It's so sweet," I said.

"And not too much mayo."

"That's how it should be done. Just a touch of mayo. People often ruin it by smothering it in mayonnaise."

"Only a few places in New York get it right."

"Do they *really* get it right?"

"A couple of places do. And they serve Maine lobster. The real deal."

"We are so going there."

He smiled at me and handed me a napkin.

"I'm a mess, aren't I?"

"You've got a bit of mayo on your chin, but I wouldn't call it ruined."

I wiped it off. "I'd say forgive me, but I'd be lying. I'm enjoying this too much. What a treat."

"Do you remember the first time you had lobster?"

"Not at all. I was lucky—we always had lobster when I was growing up. My Uncle Vaughn was a lobsterman, so we had it whenever we wanted it. My earlier years were a blur of lobster. It was ironic. We were dirt poor, but because of Uncle Vaughn, we ate like kings. Sometimes, when my uncle knew I needed to get away from his monster of a brother, he'd take me out on his boat with him. You should have seen the sheer amount of sea gulls that boat attracted. It was crazy."

"And probably unsanitary."

"You are correct. But it wasn't too bad. They mostly hung back. But there were hundreds of them. I miss those days. You would have liked my uncle. I wish he had been my father."

* * *

Later, after we'd cleaned up, we took the rest of the champagne into the living room. Alex placed it in a bucket filled with ice, and we watched the sun set over Cadillac Mountain.

"I love the Manhattan skyline, but nothing beats this," Alex said.

"It's peaceful. Look at the cars traveling up the mountain. Can you see their headlights?"

"I can."

He topped off our champagne glasses, put the bottle back in its bucket, and then lifted his arm so I could move closer to him and rest my head against his chest.

We stayed like that for several hours, and long before the sun finally dipped from sight, I knew what was coming soon for each of us. And I dreaded it. What was coming was sleep—in separate bedrooms. Something I didn't want at all.

Today had been a mix of fun and truth telling, but nothing especially romantic, though lying next to him now was nice. Still, nothing had happened between us that suggested we might end up in bed together. I wasn't seeking sex—though I wouldn't say no to it now because I was more than ready to be with him. I was seeking intimacy. We didn't come here to sleep apart. At least, I didn't. I came here to be with him in every way possible, which included sleep. I knew that when we returned to New York, the sort of paradise we were enjoying now would come to an abrupt end. While I could, I wanted to capitalize on all of our time together.

"What do you have planned for tomorrow?" I asked.

"More of this. Maybe the next day we'll go into town, shop, and have dinner somewhere. Maybe at a nice restaurant. Maybe not. A diner would do me just fine."

"Me, too. Sounds perfect."

"We should get some sleep," he said.

Reluctantly, I lifted myself off him, stood and stretched. I could feel his eyes on me, and I could sense that he also didn't want to separate. I thought about what I was going to say to him, and it was ridiculous. *See you in the morning, Alex?* Please. I decided to go there. "Would you like to sleep with me tonight?"

"As in share a bed with you?"

"Yes."

"Are you sure about that?"

"I wouldn't have asked otherwise. I don't want to be apart from you tonight. Or at all while we're here, actually. I'd be lonely in that massive bed, and I'd just be thinking of you in the other room anyway."

"So would I."

"So let's get rid of that frustration. Ready for bed?"

* * *

In the bedroom, the atmosphere shifted with anticipation.

"What side do you like to sleep on?" he asked.

"The right."

He smiled. "And there you have it. I prefer the left."

We each pulled down our corner of the bed, and then Alex cleared his throat. "I don't really know how to say this," he said.

"Say what?"

"This is awkward."

"Nothing should be awkward between us as this point."

"I generally sleep in the nude."

I felt a rush at the thought of that, but bit down hard on it. The idea of seeing him naked thrilled me. "Who's stopping you?"

"Are you sure about this?"

"I want you to be comfortable and sleep well." Even I heard my voice break when I spoke. *Holy shit, I'm going to see him naked.*

"You sound a little unsure about that."

Who knows what came over me—probably years of holding back fueled by the urgency to go forward—but for whatever reason, I pulled my tank top over my head. I tossed it onto a chair across from me, unfastened my bra, tossed it on to the chair, and then I took off the rest of my clothes, leaving on only my panties. There was only so far I could go the first time out, but to get to this point felt liberating. I stood in front of him and saw him eyeing my full breasts with clear lust and desire stamped on his face. His gaze traveled down the length of my body, which he'd never seen so exposed, and then came back to my breasts before meeting my eyes.

"You're beautiful," he said in a low voice.

I smiled with a sense of trepidation and anticipation as I waited for him to do the same. It didn't take him long to get the hint, but I wondered how far he'd take it. Just to his boxers? Or would he go all the way?

He tugged his shirt over his head and left it on the floor. Off came his jeans, also left on the floor. He hesitated for a moment, a silence stretched between us, but then he went for it and stepped out of his boxers. He flung them aside and stood before me, naked.

Just as he had appraised my breasts, I took in every inch of him, and finally saw what I knew was going to be a challenge. He was indeed large. And thick. It seemed perfectly proportioned, just like the rest of him.

And then, as I looked at it, it started to stiffen.

Before I could get a better look, I got into bed, and he followed in after me. The sheets were cool and soft. The mattress was firm and comfortable. I asked him to turn onto his side, and I pressed my nearly naked body against his back so he wasn't pressed against mine. If he was, I knew I wouldn't be able to take it. I slung my arm low over his waist and gently stroked his stomach while I kissed his shoulder. It wasn't long before the head of his penis nudged against my hand and then stretched beyond it. At that moment, I could almost feel the energy surging between us because he obviously knew what was brushing against the back of my hand. When I couldn't stand it any longer, I reached for it on impulse and, when I did so, felt my whole body turn into a silo of heat. It felt huge in my hand, as thick as a wrist, and I could feel it throbbing. The fact that I was doing this was a massive turn-on—a territory unexplored. I stroked it gently and could feel myself growing wet almost immediately.

"Jennifer," he said.

"Yes, Alex?"

"If you keep doing that...."

"I'm not about to stop now."

"Fine, then."

With a swiftness that surprised me, he swung around on the bed, flung the bedding off each of us, and straddled me with his hands pinning mine firmly against the mattress.

His cock lay heavily on my stomach. I gasped at the sudden change of position, but then, in the moonlight, I saw the look of longing on his face, and felt the urgency in his touch when he removed my panties in one quick motion.

"I hope you're not tired," he said, "because you're going to be up for hours."

"Alex—"

"I told you your first time would be special. I meant that. But you're going to need stamina for that. You're first time is going to be something you'll remember favorably for the rest of your life. I'm going to make certain of that. You'll see."

He kissed me gently on the mouth, and then harder until I could barely breathe. I felt the stubble on his chin again. It was rough against my cheek and then against my neck as he probed lower. His tongue tasted me, and his lips covered me. Low murmuring sounds came from his throat until he found one of my nipples and attended to it with his mouth.

And then he stopped.

"I've said it twice, and now I'm going to prove it to you. Without barely touching you, I'm going to make you come. And then you're going to come in other ways tonight. Throughout the night. Are you ready for that?"

I felt as if my body couldn't take much more, and we had just started, which was pathetic. I writhed beneath his touch. I struggled against it as he lowered his mouth to my ear, pressed his chest ever so lightly against my nipples, and began to rub them with his own nipples while he whispered everything he was about to do to me.

It was too much. It was sensation overload. I fought against him, but he told me it was in vain. Again and again, his nipples brushed against my own nipples. Again and again, he said unthinkable things to me. Again and again, he pushed me further to an edge I didn't know existed, but had only heard about.

But this edge was cutting. It was raw and unexpected. His chin dipped down and his stubble brushed against my naked flesh, which left me writhing on the bed to the point that I felt I was going to explode.

"Alex," I said.

He didn't respond. He just kept doing what he was doing. The same motions, over and over. Barely touching me, which seemed to me the cruelest part. I wanted his hands on me, but he was determined to deny me that. This was so close to torture that I wanted to slap him for it.

It was at that point that I became wild. I felt as if I couldn't contain myself any longer. I wanted to beat him for what he was doing to me now. I wanted to float above my body and look down at us from the ceiling so I could witness what he was doing to me. I wanted to flee. I wanted to stay. But most of all, I wanted to come.

And then, with one harsh, unexpected word, he said, "Now!"

Something I'd never felt before overtook my body and I cried out in such pleasure, it left me shaking, even when it was over. I lay there, trembling. I looked up at him, then at the darkness that was the ceiling, where I had wanted to be a moment ago, and I couldn't believe what I'd just experienced. It was beyond what I had expected. But obviously, he had more in mind.

"I told you," he said. "I can bring you to orgasm without barely touching you."

"That was incredible," I said.

"That's just the beginning."

He snaked his way down from my breasts to my belly, and then he parted my legs slightly, hesitated, and then spread my thighs wide. His head lowered from sight, but I could feel his tongue slip inside of me. I couldn't believe his mouth was down there, or what he was doing there. I couldn't believe I could ever be so open to a man. His licked my wet folds, pressed around them, and flicked them with his tongue. He tasted them for long moments before he went to my clitoris and covered his mouth over it while he sucked until I screamed out again.

"What are you doing to me?"

"Everything that you've deprived yourself of."

"It's too much."

"So you've said. And it hasn't even begun."

I heard him spit in his hand, and I knew what that meant. He was lubricating himself. I could feel his arm move backward and forward. He lifted up my hips a bit, and then he asked me if I was ready.

"If I'm not ready now, I never will be."   I couldn't help a little laugh, but it was a nervous, almost manic laugh. It was a laugh filled with the uncertainty of the unexpected. It was a laugh laced with a trace of fear.

Is this going to hurt?

I felt the tip of his cock press against me, and I was surprised that it *didn't* feel as if it was going to hurt. He pressed further into me, and it felt tight, but good. He had prepared me for this. He'd spent an hour making sure I was wet and ready for him. He knew exactly what he was doing, probably because he knew that given the size of his penis, he could cause great pain.

Slowly, inch by careful inch, he moved within me until I did feel pain. I gasped when I felt an odd sensation, a kind of giving way of flesh, and then I felt a warm moistness spread between my legs. We both knew what that meant, and for a moment he paused and his eyes searched mine, his soul a mirror of my own.

"Are you—?"

"Don't stop," I said.

He plunged deeper into me, which made me curl up and grasp him around his shoulders while he pumped into me. His rhythm was steady and strong.

He never looked away from me. I absorbed every bed-shaking thrust with a mixture of pain and pleasure, mostly the latter. Thank God for the latter. I melted into him and eventually started to meet his thrusts with my own. When I became wildly aroused, my head arched back and he barked that word again: "Now!"

The command startled me so much that I came. And then I came again. And again. Somehow, each orgasm made the moonlit room grow even darker. I threw my hands over my face while he continued to pulse inside of me, and I felt as if I was aloft, not part of my body at all. I was hovering just outside of myself, which made no sense to me because I was holding on to him fiercely for support. My grip was so strong around his shoulders that I had bound myself physically to him, but my head and my heart and my body were in the ether. I was in another place. He kept pounding and pounding, his head lowering to suck on my nipples or to bury his mouth against my lips or my ears as his sweat dripped down onto me. He was like a machine, precise and efficient. Without exhaustion, he drilled into me, always checking my expression to make sure that I was with him. How long could he last? Certainly, not that much longer.

But it was longer than I'd expected. Thirty minutes later, when his body finally shuddered as he came in a roar and we both were spent, I realized that I had no idea what I was up against.

He still was on top of me. "Now are you my girlfriend?" he said.

I didn't answer. Even though in my heart I was his girlfriend, I wasn't ready to commit to that yet. It was a loaded term for me. My father once told me that I'd never find anyone. He said that, if on the off chance that I somehow did, they'd leave me once they learned that I was nothing more than a common, filthy whore, just like my mother. It made no sense to me then, but when he was drunk, he made no sense. But his words still stuck like glue, and I was damned that even at this point in my life, I'd yet to shake them off.

My head was spinning now, but Alex wasn't about to give up.

"All right then. Too soon. But are you mine?"

"Only if you're mine."

"That equals thing again, huh?"

"I'm sorry."

"Don't apologize," he said quietly. "I'm yours. But I have been for a while now. I'm completely yours."

"Take me again."

Somehow, he did. He became erect in what seemed like seconds. Then, he slid inside of me and rode me, and I didn't know where I was or who I was when he maneuvered me around the bed into more positions than I thought were possible. But I knew that this was right. I knew that I was his and that he was mine. And I knew in some part of my being as he thrust into me and whispered things to me that were fueled by passion, that there was no turning away from this now.

As fierce as he was in bed, never once didn't I trust him. He seemed to intuitively know exactly how to position his body so I would enjoy the maximum pleasure.

We went so late into the night that I saw morning break beyond the windows in front of me. And when I came again, my body spent from the convulsions of yet another orgasm, he gently pulled out of me, turned me onto my side, and wrapped his arm around my waist as I quickly fell into a deep sleep.

CHAPTER FOURTEEN

In the morning, I woke alone. I sat up in bed and was disappointed not to see Alex beside me until I got a look at the time on the clock on the bedside table. It was nearly eleven a.m. Unbelieving, I just stared at the time. Then, feeling guilty that I'd slept so late, I pulled back the covers, and saw the bloodstains in the center of the bed. Since I was naked, I quickly dressed into the clothes I wore the day before and stripped the bed, as well as the mattress pad.

I did it all in shame even though I knew that the blood was only natural. Still, I didn't need to see it, and neither did he.

I balled up everything, and only when I saw in relief that I hadn't stained the mattress itself, did I begin to feel the pain in my body. Every part of me was sore, especially one part of me that felt as if I should send it flowers, a sympathy card and offer it a heart-felt apology.

I turned to put the bedclothes onto the floor, and saw that Alex was outside. He stood at the shoreline skipping rocks across the water. He was wearing tan-colored shorts and no shirt. Was this him as a young boy? Is this how he escaped from his parents?

I'd done the same thing as a young girl, especially when my uncle took me to the ocean for a day of lobstering. The effect of skipping stones so they sailed and bounced off water was calming to the point of being almost hypnotic.

I wondered how much else Alex hadn't told me about his past, but it would come in time. It occurred to me that I didn't know how his parents had died. How long had they been dead? How old were they when they passed? At thirty, Alex was relatively young for both parents to be deceased. Even if his mother gave birth to him at thirty-five, she'd only be sixty-five now. Far too young to be gone, unless there was an underlying issue with her health. The same was true for his father, but both dying so young? There was something there, but I shook the thought because I wanted him to tell me himself, and because

I needed to move it if I was going to look halfway decent when I saw him.

Seeing my chance for a quick shower, I dashed toward my closet, found something short and cute to wear for the day, and brought it with me into the bathroom. I closed the door, undressed, and stepped into the glass-encased shower. I turned on the water, but kept the temperature low. I was hot enough from running around.

On the shelves above me were all of the Aveda products that I used at home. Lisa must have told him what to buy. Of course she had. But what I had before me was an even broader selection than I had at home. So like a kid in a candy store, I looked at the different types of face washes, chose an exfoliant, plunged my face and head beneath the warm water until I was soaking wet, and started to wash myself. Twenty minutes later, I was dressed and my hair was dry and pulled back into a chic ponytail. On my face, I used only the lightest touch of makeup because my skin was practically glowing after last night.

When I stepped into the bedroom, I was surprised to find that the bed was made with new bedding, and that Alex was stretched out in one of the chairs. Without his shirt on and with his legs spread open wide, I had all I could do to meet his eyes.

"Good morning," he said.

God, he looks sexy.

"Good almost afternoon," I replied.

"How are you today?" he asked.

I knew why he was asking, and I blushed at the thought of an answer. "I'm good."

"Just good?"

"Maybe a little sore."

"Too sore for more?"

"Definitely not too sore for more. Give me the afternoon, and I'll be ready to go by evening."

I looked for last night's bedding, and saw that it was gone. I didn't want him to see the blood, but there was nothing I could do about that now. Somewhere in the house, he'd already started a wash while I was showering. Again, a sense of shame overcame me. I felt embarrassed.

Damn it.

I went over to him, sat in his lap, and ran my fingers through his thick hair before I kissed him. I put my arm around his bare shoulders while he caressed one of my legs with his right hand.

"Last night was beautiful," I said. "Thank you."

"Why are you thanking me?"

"Because you knew exactly what you were doing. Because it could have gone a million different ways. And because it's something I won't forget."

"Neither will I."

He smiled, but the smile didn't quite show in his eyes. He seemed distracted to me. "Is everything all right?" I asked.

"Everything's fine. Just some weirdness at work, but what else is new?"

"Anything I can do?"

"If you're as hungry as I am, there is."

"You don't know the depths of my hunger."

"By that, I'm going to assume you mean food."

"Maybe, maybe not."

He patted my ass. "When we arrived yesterday, we passed a farm stand a few miles down the street. I thought we might take a drive there and see if we can find anything that inspires us for dinner tonight. All the crops are in harvest now. There should be all sorts of great stuff—corn, tomatoes, baby potatoes, broccoli, you name it. I also noticed that they serve some sort of lunch there, though I was going too fast to see what kind of lunch. I think cheese was involved."

"You wouldn't know. You were going, like, eighty."

"So, I was. And who can blame me in a car like that? Want to give it a try?"

"The car or the farm stand?"

"The farm stand."

"Absolutely. The Whole Foods of Maine, only better. You're on." I patted his own ass as he lifted me out of the chair and stood beside me. "Grab a shirt—I don't want all the local girls feasting on you."

He went into what was supposed to be his bedroom and came out with a white polo shirt that clung to him like a second skin and somehow made him look sexier, which made no sense to me since he was a god without his shirt on.

"Don't think I won't be chasing off the locals boys if they come anywhere near you," he said.

"It could happen. Some young farming stud longing for a lass...."

"I'm prepared."

"He might need me to break in one of his new horses. One of the big ones."

"I think that happened last night."

I giggled. He reached for my hand and we started to leave.

"You know, Alex, you really should eat well today. Choose nutrient-dense foods. Here's hoping that they have something with protein of some sort. You're going to need it later tonight."

He stifled a laugh. "As if you're not. Last night was just a primer. Tonight—or hell, probably when we get back—is when things will really get interesting."

"You're such a tease."

"Really? When we get back, you'll see that I'm just telling the truth."

* * *

When we left the house and started to walk toward Alex's black Mercedes SL Roadster, which was gleaming in the mid-afternoon sun like the shiny jewel that it was, I noticed two men I hadn't seen before.

One was standing to the right of the gated entrance to Alex's property, and the other was off to the left. My first thought was that these were no ordinary men. They were guards of some sort.

Dark glasses shielded their eyes. They were completely in black, and stood just off the street, near the wooded area, where the foliage partly concealed them.

What alarmed me was that each man carried a gun in a holster low at his waist. Some sort of high-tech communication device was attached to their heads. Mikes were at the sides of their mouths. Each had an earpiece in one ear. They looked focused and serious.

"Who are they?"

Alex kept his voice light. "Security."

"Since when do we have security?"

"They arrived not long after we did yesterday." He turned to me. "You were just too distracted to notice them."

"Do you always travel with security?"

He didn't have time to answer, because the man at our right motioned him over and they began to talk. I stood by the car and tried to listen, but I couldn't hear them. An annoying breeze rustled the leaves in the trees, and Alex and the other man were speaking too lowly for me to hear what they were saying. I looked at the man to my left, who gave me a curt nod.

"Good morning, Ms. Kent."

"Good morning. Have you been out here long? Would you like some water or for us to bring you back something to eat?"

"We're fine, Ms. Kent. Thank you."

I leaned against the car while Alex continued his conversation. And then I saw another man. Across from me, down the road, was a black Range Rover parked on the side of the street. A man dressed similarly to the others stood outside the driver's side door. He also wore a gun and the same equipment around his head.

What the hell? I thought.

"Ready?" Alex asked as he jogged back toward the car.

"Absolutely. Top down?"

"Let's keep it up today. They're calling for showers."

"It's perfectly sunny, Alex."

"The weather in Maine can change on a dime. You know that. Come on. I'm starving."

We got inside and buckled up. Down the street, I saw the man next to the Range Rover step into it. When he opened the door, I saw another man sitting in the passenger's seat.

"So, this is unusual," I said. "Four guards?"

He started the car, put his hand on my thigh, and said, "Try to ignore them. They're just doing their jobs."

"To protect you from what?"

He was about to pull away, but then stopped and looked at me. "The entire time you've been with me, from that very first night at the Four Seasons, I've had protection with me. It's just that out here in the wilds, it's a lot more noticeable than it is when we're in a crowded room. It's something I do as a precaution. It's done for a reason, and you know the reason. Because of my position and my money, I'll always be a target. That's why they're here—to make sure I'm not a target. They're doing their jobs. And in case anything happens—not that it's going to—we'll be protected. OK?"

"That's going to take some getting used to. But I get it. It's just new to me, that's all." And then a thought occurred to me. "I hope they didn't hear me last night. That would be pretty embarrassing."

He put the car into gear. "We're a few hundred feet from them. I sincerely doubt that they heard anything."

"I hope you're right because I won't be holding back later."

He laughed at that, put the car into gear, and we sped off down the road, the Range Rover hot on our tail as Alex's hand dipped between my legs, cupped my sex, and gently started to stimulate me to the point that I definitely knew that I was in for it later.

* * *

The farm stand Alex noticed when we passed it the day before was a boon that brought back fond memories of me and my Aunt Marion, who was married to my Uncle Vaughn, and who was one of the great delights of my life. At seventy, she had more sauce and swagger than Beyoncé did at thirty.

She was gone now, and oh, how I missed her. When my Uncle Vaughn was out lobstering, sometimes my aunt would steal me away and, if it was late summer, we'd come to a place like this. We'd soak it all in while we walked around the fresh vegetables, fruits and herbs, and then we'd conspire on what we'd make for dinner.

Just as Alex and I were going to do now.

I looked off to my right as the Range Rover pulled alongside the Mercedes, a rush of dust spilling over it in a rolling cloud.

Nice, I thought. *And so subtle.*

I hoped to hell the men wouldn't get out, but sure enough, one did. I turned to look at him, and saw that he was scanning the dozen or so people walking through the stand, baskets in hand while they selected all the fresh produce they could handle. Some looked back at him, but he didn't seem to mind as much as they did. This was no place for the threat of a gun. Later, I'd ask Alex if they could tone it down and be more discreet.

"I think I see what you mean about the lunches they serve here," I said to him, now determined to ignore the guard so I could spend quality time with Alex. "Looks like fresh artisanal bread paninis, and they have iced tea. I'm way down for that. You?"

"Absolutely."

"Good, because I'm famished."

I went over to an older woman behind a counter and smiled at her. She was somewhere in her sixties, thickly built, and was wearing what was obviously a homemade dress made from a patterned fabric that looked light and comfortable. She had blue eyes and wore no makeup, and her graying hair was pulled away from her face in a kerchief.

"Hello," I said.

She nodded at me while I looked up at the chalkboard above her, where their menu was written. It didn't just list paninis. In the glass cooler I stood in front of, they had everything a Maine girl could want. A traditional potato salad. Macaroni and cheese they'd likely warm before serving. A French potato salad that looked divine because it was loaded with herbs and scallions, and was likely tarted up with fresh lemon and vinegar. There were heaps of sliced heirloom tomatoes, basil and rounds of homemade sheep's milk mozzarella on one large platter. And desserts were everywhere. Take your pick. They looked glorious.

Alex put his arm around my waist.

"Did you make all of this?" I asked the woman.

"Some of it. I made the salads. My sisters made most of the desserts." She pointed down at a basket filled with chocolate brownies. "Except those. I made those."

"They look delicious. It's the French potato salad that has my name on it."

"It's my mémère's recipe. I also made that."

"I've lived in Maine my whole life. It's been a while since I've been down to the Point."

"How long have you been gone?"

I didn't tell her that I'd left. What did she see in me that made her make that statement? How had I changed since I left Maine that made it so noticeable? "Just a few months."

"Still a Maine girl," she said. "And a beautiful girl. You remind me of my sister when she was young. She was the pretty one. Always off to dances. Always with a beau on her arm. It's your hair and your eyes that remind me of her. No one could keep the boys off of her. Our father didn't stand a chance."

"That's why she has me," Alex said.

The woman looked at him with a sly smile. "You're not from Maine. I saw the car you drove up in. Showy. And I can tell in other ways. So, good luck with the local boys when it comes to this one."

"Noted," he said.

I could hear the agitation in his voice, so I pressed forward. "What would you like?"

"Where do we even begin? It all looks good to me. You tell me," Alex said. "It's been a while since I've been here."

"You used to come here?" the woman asked.

"I did," Alex said. "When I was a boy. I summered here for fifteen years."

"Live on the Point, do you?"

"I do."

She glanced at me, and in that glance I saw a world of concern that wasn't unfamiliar to me. Alex and I were of two different worlds. She knew that. Being so close to the Point, she probably knew that better than I did. On this part of the coast, where the rich collided with the poor, he was what was known as a summer person, something the locals were wary of. To her, he was one of the spoiled, rich boys. And that never went over well with the locals who had to do their laundry and buy their food in order to make a living. She didn't hide her disapproval from her stony face or her eyes, and I kind of loved her for it. Her honesty was what I missed about Maine. New Yorkers were direct, but Mainers could say more with a look— or just by lapsing into silence—than by saying anything at all.

Alex and I continued to talk and to make our decision. When we were ready, I said, "OK." I looked up at the woman, who had a bemused look on her face as she watched us. I wondered if we looked like a new couple to her. I wondered if she had ever been with one of the summer boys when she was young. Is that what I saw in her eyes? A memory? A moment ago, she was engaged with us. But now she seemed to be at once looking through me and back to another time. She didn't hear me when I spoke, but I knew why. I could tell that seeing Alex and me together had brought her to another time in her life. It was right there on her face, and I saw her expression go through a mix of emotions—first happiness, then a kind of longing, then a distinct sadness. I wondered where she was and whom she was with. Where had her life taken her to bring her to this point now?

Who was the one who got away?

I gently cleared my throat, and I saw her come back into herself. We ordered our lunch—two tomato and mozzarella paninis on their artisan wheat bread, two portions of French potato salad, two unsweetened iced teas—and then we were on our way to one of the picnic tables outside.

We sat down, and Alex cast me a look. "She was odd," he said.

"Really? I thought she was great."

"Hmmm...."

"Don't you remember her?" I asked.

"From where?"

I picked up my panini before leveling him with a glance. "From your childhood. Maine women haven't changed that much, especially here on the coast. If you go into Bangor, it's different. Even more so if you make the mistake of going into Portland, which just aches in its soul to be Boston, so we won't count them as part of Maine at all, because they're not. But here? Here, it's the same. She must be familiar to you."

"I remember women like her. I also remember them not liking me very much."

"Well, you were rich. They were poor and struggling to make it. You wore fancy new clothes. They wore hand-me-downs and cleaned your new clothes so they could get a paycheck and put food on the table. They feel an ownership to the coastline they lost to those with money. They sold out for financial reasons, and because of that necessity, the coast is no longer available to them in many places. It's complicated, but as a result, years of resentment have built between the two classes."

"I can see that."

"How's your sandwich?"

"Depressing."

"I'm sorry. But this is my home. It's where I come from. I could have ended up like her, wishing I'd taken another route and had the guts to take a chance on a better life. Did you see the look in her eyes a moment ago? It was heartbreaking. She was remembering something from her past. I don't know what it was, but it was clear that it was a missed opportunity. Or something along those lines. I've seen it too many times while living here to not know that look, so I worked hard in school and then drove myself to get out of this joint with Lisa in tow. Please don't think that I'm judging her, because I'm not. She reminds me of some of my favorite stoic relatives. What's eating at me is the usual—my parents again. My father expected me to become her. Since my mother refused to ever disagree with him or anything he did to me, I assume she felt the same way. As soon as I could, I got as far away from here and them as possible."

"I'm sorry you went through that, Jennifer. Nobody deserves that."

"In a way, I'm—what's the word? It certainly isn't grateful. But in an odd way, I'm OK that I went through what I went through. Yet in a deeper way, I'm not OK with it at all. If that even makes sense. I guess what I'm saying is that what I went through with them shaped the person I am today. I wanted more for myself, so I made that happen. They'd hate it if I said to their faces that their treatment of me actually helped me."

"And left scars."

"Just as your parents left scars."

He didn't react to that. Instead, he dropped the subject and moved forward. With the focus now on him, this conversation had just ended. He picked up his sandwich, and took a bite. "Actually, this is delicious," he said. "Yours?"

I forgave him for all that he couldn't face, because I'd been there myself for too many years. I knew how difficult it was to face your past, especially where your parents were concerned. I'd never judge him for keeping quiet. I wanted to tell him that whether you're Alexander Wenn or Jennifer Kent, we all have to face the demons that affect our lives. In order to move forward, we needed to accept all the wrongs that were done to us, or else we would be stuck, just as I sensed the woman who served us was stuck. Or mired in the regrets of the past. It didn't matter. It was all the same. I was getting to a healthier space—but I had a long way to go before I crushed my own demons.

It appeared that he also did. No one knew who we really were but ourselves, especially if we denied whom that evolving person was because it was simply easier to do so. But I hoped that one day he would take the leap inward to figure out who Alex Wenn was without his parents' abuse and without the devastating loss of his wife, because a good deal of that person no longer existed.

I kept my voice light when I spoke again, the ugliness of my former life now cast to the breeze. I wasn't going to let it ruin my day.

"It's all about the tomatoes," I said, taking another bite. "And the cheese." I shrugged my shoulders as he chewed. "Oh, hell, and actually the bread."

"I'm glad you're satisfied."

"I am. I hope you are."

"I don't think you realize how satisfied I am," he said.

CHAPTER FIFTEEN

When we left the farm stand, it was with three paper sacks filled with vegetables, two bunches of sunflowers, cheeses, breads and salads, all of which somehow fit into the Mercedes' tiny trunk.

While I was putting the bags inside in such a way that it would minimize the risk of everything rolling around on our trip home, I spotted Alex speaking again with one of the guards. He was gesticulating with his hands, and I saw him show the guard his cell phone, which the guard looked at before Alex addressed him again.

Something's going on. But how far do I press it? If it had to do with business, he wouldn't consult with his security. He'd consult with his board. Or maybe with me. So what is it?

When he came back to the car, he looked tense until he saw me, and then his face brightened. But that happened a bit too quickly—it was like a switch going on—and my suspicions deepened. We each got into the car.

"Is something wrong, Alex?"

"Just the usual shit."

"What's the usual shit?"

"People," he said. "When I first met you when you interviewed for me, I told you that I wouldn't mind leaving Manhattan behind and just living in Maine. But I can't do that now, so I have to put up with distractions. All the time. Generally, I just deal with it, but I have no time for it here when I'm with you. Sorry if I sound agitated."

"Don't worry about it. Can you elaborate?"

"I'd rather not talk about it. It's being taken care of. I'm not trying to shut you out, Jennifer—that's not my intent. In fact, what I'm trying to do is just the opposite. I want to let them deal with whatever it is they need to deal with so I can let you in. Let them work through the bullshit."

What bullshit? "OK. But if you need to talk, I'm here to listen."

He started the car. "I appreciate that. And thanks for letting me vent and deal with it on my own. I came here to chill out and maximize my time with you. I plan to do that. They'll handle the rest."

The rest of what?

* * *

When we got back to his place, we pulled beneath the shade of an elm tree and unpacked the trunk. One of the guards wanted to talk to Alex, but he instructed the man to talk to the other guard, who just now was parking up the street in his Range Rover.

"Scott just briefed me," he said. "Jennifer and I don't want to be disturbed for the rest of the day unless it's critical. Understood? Critical."

"Yes, sir."

"Thank you, Ben."

What could be critical?

Bags in hand, we went inside the house. While Alex unloaded the groceries into the already packed refrigerator, I stood over the sink and clipped the ends of the sunflowers with a pair of scissors I found in a drawer.

"Do you have a large vase?" I asked.

"Absolutely."

He left the kitchen, came back with one, and kissed me on the back of my neck. I arranged the flowers, filled the vase with water, and then admired the bouquet on the sideboard before I brought it to the dining room and placed it in the center of the long, rectangular table.

Alex came up behind me and put his arms around my waist. "It's beautiful," he said.

"I love sunflowers."

"Would you like to take a walk with me on the beach?"

"I'd love to."

We walked down the wooden stairs that led to the shoreline, and started off to the right. Even with the breeze coming off the ocean, it was still early enough in September to be comfortable in shorts and a light shirt. I looked well ahead of us, and noticed for the first time that there seemed to be no other houses after Alex's.

"How much of the beachfront is yours?" I asked.

"Pretty much as far as you can see."

I turned to him. "You own all of this?"

"My parents did, so I guess now I do."

I wanted to ask him how his parents died, but I also wanted to keep the mood light after the earlier tension. I'd wait for him to tell me himself. I knew I could Google it, but that felt invasive to me. He'd tell me when he was ready.

I reached for his hand, he grasped it tightly in his own, and he pulled me close to him. I wasn't sure what I felt when his fingers closed over mine—a needing, a wanting—but it was meaningful. Something was happening to him now that he didn't want to discuss with me. I needed to respect his privacy, just as I would expect him to respect mine if there was something I didn't want to talk about. But at his level, our problems were worlds apart. I couldn't imagine what it might be, but it was significant. I hadn't seen him like this before. This was different from the tension brought on by too much work. This was something else.

We walked for about ten minutes before nature eventually did its thing. Gradually, I felt him begin to relax. His hand didn't hold so tightly onto mine; instead, it softened against mine. I heard him take a deep, cleansing breath, and then it was just the two of us with the ocean lapping against the shore or crashing into rocks in the background. Seagulls sailed overhead with a cacophony of calls. I let go of his hand, reached behind me, released my ponytail, and shook out my hair. It immediately picked up the breeze and it felt wonderful. He watched me as I did it, and I could sense a shift in him.

He stopped and turned to me. "I'm sorry about today."

"I know you're under some kind of pressure. When you want to tell me, tell me. There's no need to apologize."

"Thank you for that.

"There's no need to thank me."

"It's just that sometimes things in my life can go to shit in an instant. I have no control over it. I'll say it again because it bears repeating. The only thing I want during this week is to be with you and to have some normalcy with you." He bent down, took my face in his hands, and kissed me hard on the lips. "And I want to make love to you, Jennifer. Now."

I wished he wouldn't use the word 'love', but there was no stopping him. Until I knew that what we had was real, and that it was indeed love that was growing between us, I prefered that he just say he wanted to be with me. That was better. That made my own demons happier. Otherwise, it was confusing to me and to them. My trust issues kicked in, and my barriers went up.

But I wasn't going to let them get the best of me. Not now. Not after last night, and not after that confession.

"You want to do it here?" I asked.

"Why not?"

"Because we're out in the open."

"And that doesn't interest you?"

There was a dare in his voice that I instantly responded to. I rarely passed on a dare. I looked around us. There didn't appear to be a soul in sight, but that didn't mean that one of his guards wasn't lurking within the tree line. "What if somebody sees us?"

"What if they do?"

"We could be arrested."

"This is private property. Come over here. It's dry. No hard rocks, just fine gravel and some sand. Come."

Today had been such a mixed bag of weirdness. I had expected this to come later, not so early in the afternoon. And certainly not here. But I wanted it. I wanted it to be like it was last night when we were connected and before I knew that something was troubling him, and that men were guarding him and his property for some reason unknown to me. I wanted to get us back on course. So I followed him away from the ocean toward the edge of the trees. I sat down and looked up at him. The sun shone against his back, and cast his features in deep shadow.

"Take off your shirt," he said.

"Take off your pants."

"Shirt first."

"We do this together, or not at all," I said.

"So, we're always going to be on equal ground?"

"Maybe not always—it'll likely fluctuate—but right now we are."

"Fine. Then, shirt for shirt."

"I'm up for that." *I'm so not up for this.*

I pulled my shirt over my head, and he did the same. He laid his shirt down just to the left of me, and then took my shirt and laid it just below his, making a blanket of sorts.

"Stand up," he said.

I did.

"Turn around."

I did what I was told.

He brushed the sand off my ass and then asked me to sit on our shirts. "No sand that way. You won't want any of that when I enter you."

My lips parted at that, but I said nothing.

"To be fair, you need to take off your bra. Then we'll be even."

I hesitated, but then I removed it, and I couldn't help but feel a chill of anticipation mixed with the unexpected thrill of exposure. How did he know exactly what to do to me to make me feel that thrill? Was I so easily read? Was I that obvious? I never thought I was, but he clearly knew what he was doing with me, and how far he could go with me. He pushed right up against my self-imposed line of 'don't go any further.' Then he pressed it to the edge, and took it a bit further so I was just outside of my comfort zone, but not so far out of it that I became uncomfortable. He was wickedly evil that way, but I'd be lying if I said it wasn't a turn on. Alex took me to the point where I was nervous as hell, but not in such a way that I felt compelled to flee. It was a balancing act that he'd mastered.

And I was his servant.

He took off his shorts, and I saw that he was wearing no underwear, which surprised me. His cock, long and flaccid, hung beautifully between his legs. I thought it was perfect, and now, in the daylight and despite him being in shadow, I certainly had a better view of it than I did last night. Seeing it was enough to inflame me with desire. I wanted to reach out and touch it, but I knew he'd have none of that until I was completely naked.

"Now, your shorts," he said roughly.

I removed them and saw the look of disbelief that crossed his face when he noticed that I wasn't wearing panties. Feeling brazen, I spread my legs for him and leaned back, bracing myself with my arms on his shirt. I was already wet. I knew he could tell, and his face darkened as he took in the length of my body.

Wordlessly, he sank to his knees and carefully placed his hands on his shirt so they'd collect no sand. He met my eyes for a moment. A hint of a smile appeared on his lips, and then with a force I wasn't expecting, he buried his mouth between my legs.

He entered me with his tongue, which caused me to arch my back in ecstasy and then writhe in excitement as the stubble on his chin did things to me that just intensified the act. He covered my clit with his mouth, sucked and nibbled on it, and drove me to orgasm faster than I had expected. It was still an alien sensation to me—how could I have betrayed myself this gift for so long?—but I had my reasons for doing so, and I didn't regret them. There was a reason I was with Alex now. There was a reason why he'd taken my virginity, and there was a very good reason why he was close to bringing me to the edge again. He was rubbing his chin over my clit in little swirling motions, which made me want to reach out and stop him because the pleasure was almost too much. His hooded eyes looked up to meet mine, and between us was a fire that burned until I exploded again.

I fell back on the shirts, but he wasn't done with me yet. Now his mouth was on mine. I could taste myself on him, and then, just as meticulous as he'd been last night, he started to work his way down my body. He lowered his head to service my breasts, which he tended to tirelessly until he pressed a finger inside of me and told me to squeeze myself around it. I did, and he began to probe deep. First one finger, then another. And finally another. I felt full and on the verge again. His thumb lightly started to rub my clit, and I was gone. I shook my head at him as a wave crashed somewhere inside of me.

"I can't do it again," I said.

"You will."

"Give me a　"

"Come!"

I did, and it was more powerful than the last one. I closed my eyes, and felt him withdraw his fingers. And then it was he who was inside of me. He started to thrust in long, slow strokes, nudging up his body each time he came forward to make sure that he made contact with the most sensitive part of my sex. His eyes slipped over me with such an intensity that I couldn't look at him. I turned my head to the side, and felt his hand gently turn it back so I was looking directly at him under my lashes.

"Don't turn away."

"It's too much."

"Let yourself go."

I felt the pit of my stomach fall away as I did so. I felt weightless as he drove into me. I heard the guttural sounds he made, felt his hot breath against my skin, listened to the sounds of the seagulls soaring above us, and I went up with them. I opened my legs wider and started to meet each of his thrusts in earnest with my own.

"That's right," he said.

I pounded myself against him. I dug into the sand on either side of me with a fierceness I didn't know I had within me. I wanted to make him come. I wanted to make him feel what I already had felt four times. I lifted myself on my elbow, and wrapped my free hand around his neck. I gripped it, and pulled myself toward him.

"Come on," I said.

"What's that?"

"Faster," I said.

"What's that?"

"Fuck me," I said.

I'd never used that word with him before, but we were nothing if not primal right now, and I could tell that it excited him.

"So, it's that?" he said. "You want me to fuck you?"

"That's right, you son of a bitch. Fuck me."

I clutched myself around his penis, and squeezed with everything I had within me. I brought his head down to mine, and we kissed deeply, meaningfully. This time it was my tongue that went down his throat. He moaned when he was nearly out of breath, but I held him longer, only pulling back when I needed to. I pressed my mouth against his ear and said, "That's right. Come on, Alex. Fuck me."

"Stop—"

"Fuck me harder."

"Jennifer—"

"Don't be a pussy about it. Come on! I'm not going to break!"

And then it was on. For the next several minutes, he was on fire, and so was I. In the heat of it, I wasn't sure if I could take what I'd asked for, but I did. I kept at it. I kept pace with him. I pushed myself forward as he slammed into me, and bit his nipple so hard that that was it. He held my head there—and kept driving into me—and then he came inside of me to the point that he spilled out of me and onto my shirt.

He collapsed on top of me, and I held him close. I was panting. So was he. And then I started to giggle. He lifted his head and looked up at me as my giggle turned into a howl of laughter.

He had a grin on his face when he said, "Why are you laughing?"

"Are you serious? That was one of the best moments of my life. I'm giddy. Good God, I had no idea it would be like this."

"It wouldn't be," he said. "Not with just anyone."

"I wouldn't know."

"Trust me."

I caught my breath and kissed him on the lips. His face and his hair were sweaty. "I trust you, Alex. I hope you know what it means for me to say that. I don't say it lightly."

"I know you don't. And I'm grateful for it. I'm falling for you, Jennifer."

Please, don't say it.

"You're mine?" he asked.

That I could deal with. "You know I am. Why do you keep asking?"

"Because I need to make sure," he said. "I don't want you to go, regardless of what comes."

"What's going to come?"

"Nothing I can't handle," he said.

"What does that mean?"

"It's nothing for you to worry about. I just need to know that you're mine."

I reassured him that I was, but even then, I knew that on some level, especially after today with the presence of his security detail, he was trying to protect me from something. From what, I didn't know. But it scared me. Something was happening, and I had no knowledge of it or control over it. I held him close to me, and we just lay there, naked and spent, until we finally pulled ourselves together, dressed and left for the house.

* * *

Later that evening, after we had a dinner of tomatoes, zucchini, peppers, garlic, carrots and baby potatoes that were tossed in olive oil, roasted at a high temperature, and then tossed again with herbs from the farm stand, we relaxed in the living room, which faced the mountains and the ocean beyond.

Alex poured us each a glass of Pinot Grigio, and we enjoyed it in silence, watching the cars curve around Cadillac Mountain, but also lost in our own thoughts about what had been an unnerving and exciting day.

We started the day with a security detail I knew nothing about, we had a lunch that was fun despite the guard watching over us, and then we'd been together for our second time, this time fully out in the open on the beachfront Alex owned.

Twice that evening, Alex was called upon to join his security team outside. Each time he returned, he was filled with apologies, but no information as to what was happening. I didn't engage him. If we were going to be a couple, this was a test. Eventually, he needed to tell me what was going on. I was waiting for him to do that.

But he didn't that night.

When he was called outside a third time and offered no explanation when he left me, I was over it. I went upstairs to our bedroom, put on a tank top and some shorts, and went to sleep while he dealt with whatever it was he didn't want me to know.

When he came to bed, I was aware of his presence when he quietly stepped into the room and removed his clothing. But when he slipped beneath the sheets, I began to breathe deeply in an effort to convince him that I was asleep and not to be bothered. I felt him kiss me on the shoulder, then on my neck. And then I felt him turn onto his side. He draped his arm over me and held me close, and I felt his affection. I wanted to turn and to kiss him goodnight, but I was too disappointed that he wouldn't share with me what was an obvious situation.

Or was it?

I opened my eyes and stared into the darkness. Maybe this is just how he lived. I didn't know. I felt confused. He was a billionaire. Was someone targeting him? Was that it? If that was it, was that normal for him? I just wished he'd come clean with me and tell me, even though I felt he was protecting me from the truth by saying nothing. Maybe, at this point in our relationship, he didn't want me to know what his life really was like. Maybe he thought it would frighten me away.

So many maybes, I thought. Then I closed my eyes and went to sleep.

* * *

When morning came, so did bad news. We were headed back to Manhattan. For whatever reason, our trip to Maine had been cut short.

"I'm sorry," Alex said when he told me we were leaving.

"Two days are better than none, I suppose."

"Thank you for understanding."

I decided it was time to go there. "I don't understand. You've told me nothing. But something is going on. I'm no fool, Alex. I'm not going to pry into your life, just as I expect you not to pry into mine. But

I was looking forward to spending a week with you. I'm not going to pretend that I'm not disappointed."

"I apologize."

"It's fine. I'll be happy to see Lisa and the new apartment. I need to proof her book, which is finished, and which I promised I'd do for her. I assume you'll allow me to take these next five days off since we were going to take them off anyway?"

"Of course. If you need longer, you can have whatever time you need. I just hope you'll see me during that time."

"It depends on how quickly I can proof her manuscript. She means the world to me, and that's one person I'll never let down. But I'll be finished in time to report to Wenn on schedule. At that point, I hope you've settled whatever issue you're going through now."

I knew what I said sounded cold, but I couldn't help it at this point. He considered me his girlfriend. If something significant was happening, he should trust me enough to tell me what it was. Why he didn't was beyond me.

And then I checked myself. *This* coming from a person who had major trust issues of her own? *This* coming from the person who wouldn't verbally commit to being his girlfriend? Since I hadn't committed, why should he share anything personal with me? Maybe he just wanted to keep it private for now, and then tell me later when things settled down. His life was bigger than mine. It always would be. I either needed to be fine with that, or, to be fair to both of us, I needed to fully commit to him or end this.

The latter wasn't going to happen. I was too fond of him to let go now, so I just needed to suck it up and understand that his life with all of the complications that came with it was on a much higher level than mine. Dating Alex wasn't going to be like dating someone who had a normal life. This was a completely different arena, and I needed to be prepared to either go with it gracefully—or bow out of it gracefully.

I opted for the former, and apologized to him.

An hour later, we were back on a plane to New York. He asked if I'd like to sit next to him. But I chose to sit in the seat across the aisle from him because I had a feeling that he'd rather be alone. I also needed to come to terms with what being with him was going to be like. Once I wrapped my head around that and accepted it, things would be easier.

Once we had lifted off, it was a silent trip home with neither of us engaging each other along the way. I kept my head lowered to my Kindle and attempted to read a new thriller, but I was too distracted to see the words on the page. I was trying to read a situation that was escaping me, and I was failing to do so. I glanced over at him a few times. His nose was buried in his laptop while he typed furiously. What was he writing? Who was he writing to? And what was going on now that caused us to leave five days early?

CHAPTER SIXTEEN

It was mid-morning when we arrived at La Guardia, and despite it being September, the air nevertheless was humid when we departed the plane. Two men, whom I knew on sight were part of Alex's security team, greeted us. Alex acknowledged them with a nod, but he didn't speak to them. At least not in my presence.

We left the airport and stepped outside where a limousine was waiting to take us into the city. Two black Cadillac Escalades were parked behind the limo. I watched the two men step inside one of them, and the SUVs followed us as we pulled into traffic.

I didn't comment on anything I saw. Instead, I removed my cell phone from my handbag and texted Lisa. "Home in 30."

"If that was to Lisa, please give her my best."

"I will when I get home."

"I'll make this up to you," he said.

"There's no need to."

"Yes, there is."

"We can talk about that at some other time."

"Are you angry with me?"

"No."

"But you're distant."

"I'm just disappointed."

"Would you sit closer to me?"

I looked at him, and saw that he was at once distracted, tense and apologetic. Everything he was going through was reflected in his features, especially his eyes. How could I deny him? I scooted over to him and leaned my head against his shoulder, which had a calming effect I hadn't expected. He put his arm behind my back and held me close. Physically, he was a strong man, which was one of the things that attracted me to him.

Strong and silent, I thought. *Especially now.*

When we crossed the bridge into Manhattan, I knew our time together was closing in, so I took his hand in mine and kissed him on the cheek. "Thank you for a wonderful time," I said. "Regardless of how brief it was, I'll never forget it for many reasons." I shrugged. "What can I say, Alex? Being with you spoiled me. I wanted those five extra days with you. I won't apologize for that. I loved being with you. It's that simple."

"I wanted them as much as you did. When can I see you again?"

"Soon."

"How soon?"

"Call me when you have things under control, or I'll see you at Wenn on Monday morning. We can always talk at night."

When we approached my apartment on Fifth, the car pulled to the left and I looked up through the window at my beautiful new home. I stepped out when the car stopped, and without looking back at Alex when he reluctantly released me from his embrace, I walked across the busy sidewalk with my handbag slung over my shoulder. I gave the doorman a little wave with my fingers when he opened the door for me, and with a heavy heart that now was unexpectedly filled with sadness, confusion and longing, I disappeared from Alex's sight.

* * *

To my delight, Lisa was waiting for me in the lobby. When she saw me, she leaped out of one of the stylish chairs in the center of the cavernous space and hurried over to me. It had only been a couple of days, but I'd missed her terribly, and we hugged each other fiercely when we had crossed the distance between each other.

"So much for a week," she said.

"So much for a week," I sighed.

"Are you all right?"

"We'll talk upstairs. Not here. Is it too soon for a martini?"

"Girl, please."

"I can't wait to see what you've done to the place. If I know you, it'll be perfection."

She started to speak, but hesitated. I knew her too well not to catch that look. "What's the problem?" I asked.

"There isn't a problem. At least, I don't *think* there's a problem. You'll be the judge of that."

"What does that mean?"

"Pretty much everything you're about to see? It wasn't me."

I pressed a button for one of the elevators and looked at her. "What does that mean?"

"Let's just say you're not going to believe it when you see it."

"Alex," I said.

"Who else?"

"He had the place decorated for us, didn't he?"

"Um, yeah. You could say that. You also could say that's an understatement."

* * *

When we entered the apartment, it was like entering another space—one I didn't recognize from the last time I was here when the penthouse was empty.

Lisa and I walked from room to room, and I just took it all in, knowing that he'd done it out of kindness, and also knowing that I'd never be able to keep him from extending his generosity. To his core, that's who he was. As difficult as it was for me to accept it, I needed to learn to accept it and appreciate it.

"It's beautiful," I said.

"I was hoping you'd say that."

"Look at these Persian rugs."

"Real."

"And these paintings. I love the way they pop against the gray walls."

"Real."

I moved into the dining room and saw a clutch of sunflowers sitting in a unique vase I recognized on sight. Seeing the sunflowers was enough to make me catch my breath because of the message they sent after Alex and I had purchased sunflowers ourselves at the farm stand on the Point. The vase was another treasure. "I know why the sunflowers are here, but this vase is ridiculous. It's Lalique. It's their Bacchantes vase. It's one of their most celebrated pieces. And it looks as if it's antique."

"That's because it is. Rene himself signed it. I checked the bottom when it arrived. His name is carved there."

"That's worth a fortune."

"What isn't? Have a look around. And by the way, what's the significance with the sunflowers?"

"We bought sunflowers at a farm stand on the Point, but that was just yesterday. When did these arrive?"

"This morning."

Oh, Alex.

"Come look at your bedroom."

We went to it, and found that apparently I now had a massive, king-sized sleigh bed crafted in deep mahogany and covered with rich, glorious bedding that complemented the light green walls and the maple flooring.

I stepped into the room, looked around, and noticed that on the nightstand to the right side of my bed—where Alex knew I slept—was a black-and-white photograph of him framed in silver.

It was a portrait of him wearing a tuxedo, which he knew I loved him in, so even this was intentional.

What I was witnessing wasn't just some random designer coming in here and taking control with his or her own vision and tastes. Somehow, at some point, Alex had designed much of this with me in mind. He must have directed as much of this as he could from Maine, though I wasn't sure when or how. Had he done it late at night when I was asleep? Or that morning I slept so late? Did he order the sunflowers from the plane when he was on his computer? It didn't matter. There were too many personal touches throughout the apartment to be just something he dumped money into without giving it serious thought. I felt touched by the gesture. I felt guilty for walking away from him so cooly a moment ago.

"You need to see my bedroom," Lisa said.

We went to it. It was beautifully finished, but what she brought me to was the movie poster of the original version of "Dawn of the Dead." The director, George A. Romero, had signed it, and it featured a massive zombie head rising in the background. It was an original, probably bought at auction, and he'd had it framed.

"Can you believe it?" she asked.

"Are you going to be able to sleep with that thing in here?"

"Girl, please."

I looked at the poster, which was on the wall to the left of her bed, near the window, and I admired it not only because of what it meant to Lisa, which was a great deal, but because of what it represented. He was acknowledging that this was Lisa's and my home. By giving her this poster, he'd gone out of his way to make sure that we both knew that he knew that.

"So, I have to ask you," I said. "Did a certain person oversee this?"

She smiled at me.

"Blackwell?" I asked.

"The legend herself."

"You know, when I first met her, I didn't like her. She was really rude, dismissive and caustic with me. But things have changed. Time and again since then, she's gone out of her way for me."

Lisa looked carefully at me. "She's paid to."

"I think it's more than that."

She thought about that for a moment, and then reconsidered. "Actually, that was pretty cynical of me. We all had a fine time looking at this apartment. And then we had a great lunch and a fun conversation, which was loose and freewheeling, but not fake. Though I have to say that she is venomous if you eat anything other than salad."

"Tell me about it. But she is who she is, and I kind of love her for it. She's a straight shooter. We both appreciate that. She did a great job here."

"Over a two-day period, she put about thirty hours into what you see. She was tireless. At one point, I think there must have been twenty people in here. She was on the phone a lot, too. I think she was speaking to Alex."

"I know she was," I said.

* * *

"Martini?"

"Yes, please," I said.

In the living room, I fell into a chic, comfortable sofa. Beyond the massive expanse of windows was the Park. At this height, the view made you pause and realize that in this city, there was a greater design that you didn't necessarily see from the street. The trees—still green here even though they had begun to turn in Maine—were magnificent. I wondered how any of this could be. For months, we'd lived in a shitty little prison camp of an apartment on East Tenth Street, and now we were in a penthouse on Fifth Avenue. It didn't make sense to me, but I was grateful for it.

Within days, I'd also need to earn it.

Lisa came out of the kitchen with two martini glasses filled with what Russians called their "dear little water," which, in this case, was coddled with olives and vermouth. We touched glasses, Lisa sat next to me, and we sipped.

"I know this is selfish, but I'm glad you're home."

"Miss me?"

"More than you know."

"I missed you, too. More than *you* know."

She looked slyly at me. "What else are you missing?"

"If you're talking about my virginity, it's history."

"I knew it! Spill."

I told her everything.

"You did it on the beach?"

"We did."

"But you could have been caught."

"It was a private beach."

"Who are you?"

"Apparently, someone who is tired of being me. Or, at the very least, *that* side of me. Not the root of who I am. I'd never change that for anyone. But he's awakened something inside of me. That's for sure."

"What was it like?"

"After the eighth or tenth orgasm?"

"In one night?"

"No, between those two days, silly."

"Poor baby."

"Nobody's frowning here."

"How was he?"

"I have nothing to compare him to, but I'd say he knows exactly what he's doing. It was wonderful. I'm glad that I waited as long as I did. It made it more meaningful, especially because he knew that at my age, I wasn't giving myself away lightly. He understood that, and he respected it. But now things are weird."

"How so?"

I told her about guards appearing out of nowhere and all that unspooled from that moment, which culminated in us leaving Maine five days sooner than expected.

"Something's going on," she said. "Did he tell you what it was?"

"Not a word."

"Why?"

"I don't know. Maybe it's private. I'm a private person, so I respect his privacy. And we've only been together a short while, so he really owes me nothing, especially went I won't commit to being his girlfriend. Am I worried for him? Absolutely. Has it affected my mood? Sure it has. Am I disappointed that I wasn't able to spend the full seven days with him? Yep. But that's just me being selfish, which I pretty much need to get over if we're going to be together."

"When are you seeing him again?"

"I told him that once I had proofed your book, I'd be available to see him. There are two people in my life, Lisa—you and him. I'm not going to let you down."

She took a sip of her martini and turned to look at me on the sofa as she tucked her legs beneath her slender body. When she spoke, her tone was serious. "Jennifer, if you continue on with him, we'll still be best friends until the last zombie drops, but you need to be realistic about this. I am. I know that if you two become closer, I will have less and less time with you, just as you had with me when I was involved with my hideous exes. And I'm fine with that because it makes me happy that you've finally found someone. Don't worry about me."

"I'll never not worry about you."

"Fine. Then worry about me, but live your life. You know me. I'm a springboard. And I'm actually feeling that enough time has passed for me to start thinking about dating again."

I brightened at that. "You know, I asked Alex if he had any friends he might introduce you to."

"Oh no you didn't."

"Oh yes I did."

"Are they as hot as he is?"

"Who knows? What I do know is that good-looking guys tend to hang out with good-looking guys. We've seen that time and again. They're drawn to each other, like a Chippendale to a flame."

"An odd way to put it, but an indisputable fact."

"He mentioned one guy named Michael."

"What does he do?"

"No idea. But Alex did say that this Michael guy is way over the dating scene, and he wants what Alex wants—a relationship. He's looking for the right woman, but not finding her."

"Sign me up!"

"Alex suggested that we four have dinner at some point."

"I'm down with it."

"But we need to get your book out first. Are you happy with it?"

She blushed, but she usually did when she spoke about her own work, especially if she was pleased with it. "I think it's good."

"When can I read it?"

"You can read it now on your Kindle."

"How can I read it on my Kindle when I haven't proofed it yet?"

"OK, so here we go. When Blackwell arrived the first morning, she saw the manuscript on our old coffee table. Without even asking me, she read a few pages and asked me if I'd like her to give it to one of the editors at Wenn Publishing. She said she'd have it copy edited and proofed with comments within twenty-four hours. And she did—I got it back yesterday. Whoever she gave it to was amazing and thought of things I hadn't thought of. I worked all last night to make changes and then I uploaded the book late, late, last night. It's now live on Amazon."

"Two days, and the whole world changes."

"Are you upset that I didn't let you read it first?"

"Lisa, you just had a professional editor edit your book for you. No, I'm not upset. I'm thrilled for you. That just doesn't happen to most independent authors. I can't wait to read it. How is it doing?"

"Last I checked, it was climbing the list, so we'll see. I don't want to look again until later today. I just need to chill out about it now and let it do its thing."

"I'm proud of you. That's a big accomplishment."

"Now, I need to start the next one. As in tomorrow."

"And I need to call Blackwell to thank her for all that she's done here, and also for being kind enough to make that happen for you. Give me a second."

I went into the kitchen and pulled my phone out of my handbag. I scrolled through my contacts, found Blackwell's direct line, and called it.

She answered on the second ring.

"Jennifer," she said.

"Hello, Ms. Blackwell."

"I'm sorry about Maine."

"So, am I."

"I've talked to Alex, and I know he's determined to make it up to you."

"It's not necessary."

"Yes, it is. And we both know it, so let's just be honest with each other and leave it at that. How do you like your apartment?"

"That's one of the reasons I'm calling. You have the most amazing taste. I can't tell you how unexpected this was or how lovely it is. I know you worked very hard to accomplish what you accomplished. I wanted to thank you personally for that."

"It was my pleasure. You know I love style—whether it's squeezing that ass of yours into couture, or designing your apartment for you. Doesn't matter. It's in my blood. I couldn't bear the thought that you'd end up with some bullshit crap from Crate & Barrel. God! I'm assuming you noticed a few touches that I had nothing to do with?"

"I did."

"He might be preoccupied now, but he's thinking of you. You need to know that."

I wanted to ask her what was preoccupying him, but I didn't. That would put her in a tough spot, and frankly, it needed to come from Alex himself. "I also wanted to thank you for what you did for Lisa."

"Also my pleasure. Those editors over at Wenn Publishing mostly just sit on their asses and dream about writing their own books, which will never happen. It's pathetic. They're lazy motherfuckers. I wanted to give one of them some work, and I have to say that she came through. I hope Lisa was happy with the finished product."

"She was thrilled."

"Perfect. She's a nice girl. And by the way, I'm glad you called, because I was going to call you. Alex has an opportunity to go to an event tonight. He'd like you to join him. Are you free?"

My excuse to say no had been taken away from me—Lisa's book was edited and now online. But I was exhausted and couldn't imagine going through the maelstrom of shopping that was required for these events. I told Ms. Blackwell so.

"I've got that covered," she said.

"What do you mean?"

"Silly girl. With two dresses behind you, I now have your measurements. I made phone calls. I now have a whole rack of dresses and gowns right here for you. Also, shoes. Wait until you see the shoes. They are divoon, divoon, divoon. All you need to do is come to me at, say, six tonight, and we'll find something suitable. Bernie is on standby to do your hair and makeup because he adores you. And then you can be with Alex tonight, which I think is important."

"You do love to meddle, don't you?"

"I'm just encouraging what I believe should happen, Jennifer. There's a difference."

"What's the event?"

"It's a birthday celebration for Henri Dufort."

"The businessman?"

"To put it lightly. Dufort is into everything, particularly emerging media, which is one of the places where Wenn wants to grow. Alex has been trying to get a moment alone with Dufort for months, but the man is so busy, he's unreachable. This could be Alex's moment. He thinks you might be able to help."

"He didn't mention any of this to me this morning."

"That's because he didn't know anything about it until he got back. Naturally, he's going to the party. He has to. He said he'd like you to go with him. Will you?"

"Why didn't he call me himself?"

"He's busy right now. Will you come?"

"I work for Wenn," I said. "Of course I will. I'll see you at six."

"Thank you," Blackwell said. "And Jennifer. Don't you dare eat anything before you get here."

"I was considering a bag of chips."

"If you do, I will personally get in my car—"

"—and eating a large pizza—"

"—and drive over—"

"I'm just joking. I'll see you soon."

I hung up the phone and stood in the kitchen. *And the day just keeps getting stranger*, I thought.

I told Lisa what was happening, grabbed my martini, went into my bedroom, and started the computer on the desk that faced a window overlooking the Park. Once online, I Googled everything I could about Henri Dufort. And as I read article after article, what I learned about him and his media empire not only gave me insight into the man and what drove him to create his empire, but also into possible ways for Wenn to partner with him—if the right kind of deal was struck in such a way that it appealed to Dufort's beginnings as a young entrepreneur.

CHAPTER SEVENTEEN

After arriving by limo at Wenn, I went to Blackwell's offices on the fifty-first floor, and found her sitting at her desk crunching a mouthful of ice.

"Sorry," she said after she swallowed. "Dinner."

"So healthy of you."

"So smart of me. You should learn."

I shook my head at her as she sprang out of her seat and came over to me.

"Turn around," she said.

I turned around.

"You look good. I went through two sleepless nights thinking that you were in Maine eating deep-fried everything. All the dresses I ordered for you were custom made to your previous measurements.

Not your post-Maine measurements. I thought for sure you'd come back fat. I'm telling you, I couldn't sleep thinking what you were doing to your body."

"I also had a few sleepless nights," I said. "If we were girlfriends, I'd tell you exactly what was done to my body."

She pointed her finger at me. "You're a wicked girl, Jennifer Kent. And wipe that smile off your face—that's just too much information. I can deal with a lot, but I can't deal with that. I told you he's like a nephew to me." She lifted her eyes to meet mine. "And he also happens to be ecstatic that you agreed to go with him tonight."

"Why wouldn't I go? With Lisa's book finished, I'm essentially free. He's my employer. Of course I'd go with him."

She sat on the edge of her desk. "What's upsetting you?"

"You know what's upsetting me."

"Some things Alex just needs to deal with on his own."

"I understand that."

"No. I don't think you do."

"There were guards there. Naturally, I'm worried about him."

"I understand that. But Alex is an adult, and he'll take care of what's preoccupying him. Look. If you're going to be in a relationship with him, you're going to need to give him time to acclimate and be patient with him along the way, just as he is being patient with you. In a way, this also is new to him. It's been four years since Diana's death. If you think you're the only one taking a risk with your heart, I'm here to tell you that's not the case. He also is. You're not alone in this, so stop behaving as if you are. Don't forget that."

"Sometimes, I wish I had your perspective on life."

"That will never happen."

I rolled my eyes.

"But if I'm being completely honest? Sometimes, I wish I had your looks. But we can't have it all, now can we?"

"Probably not."

"That's the wisest thing that's come out of your trap since you got here."

"Can we go and look at the dresses?" I asked, wanting to change the subject. "I'm dying to see what you've been up to."

"You *are* going to die. The sheer art of couture doesn't even come close to describing what I've had tailored for you. Come this way. Into your changing room. It's all there, including the shoes."

I followed her into the conference room we used as a makeshift dressing and makeup room.

"Is this birthday party a high-end affair?"

"High end? You have no idea how high end. Everyone will be there, and by that, I mean anyone who matters in New York at this very moment. To Henri, that number comes down to just one hundred people, which means he has snubbed and pissed off thousands of others. Not that he cares. His guests were invited to bring one guest each. So, expect a crowd of two hundred, half of which you'll know on sight because of that business mind of yours. To date, this will be, by far, the most influential crowd you'll interact with. You'll need to be quick. Potential deals will be everywhere tonight, particularly the one he wants to make with Dufort. Alex is really going to be leaning on you. Not only to help him with Dufort, but also to think fast on your feet if you see a potential relationship for Wenn with someone else on that rooftop."

"Rooftop?"

"The party is being thrown on the top of Dufort's building on Fifth. He has the full-floor penthouse, and, since he owns the building, he also owns the rooftop. And just wait until you see that rooftop. It's been turned into one of the most glorious gardens in the city. There will be flowers and foliage everywhere. Dramatic lighting. Enviable views of the city. Intoxicating."

"Now I'm excited."

"The dresses and the shoes should excite you."

"They do. And so does the idea of that rooftop. But none of it excites me as much as making deals on the fly. That's the life I've always wanted. I want to leave now."

"Obviously, you'll have to wait." She plucked a dress from the rack beside her and held it up to me. "Here. I think it's this one."

It was a simple yet elegant black dress with beautiful lines but no frills. It was nothing like the *Gatsby* dress. No sparkle. Very little glamour. Nothing about it drew attention to itself, with the possible exception of the sexy, plunging neckline.

"Why so plain?" I asked.

She looked affronted. "Plain? It's not plain. It's understated."

"Then why so understated?"

"Because tonight, you're a businesswoman. A successful one. Your hair with be done up in a loose chignon, and your makeup with be subtle, save for the lip, which will be bright red because you do, after all, want to receive some attention. The only jewelry you'll wear are these."

She opened two boxes for me from Tiffany. In one was a pair of large diamond studs. In the other was a lovely tennis bracelet. Both had the sort of brilliant stones that would suggest I'd achieved a large measure of success. But with nothing at my neck or on my fingers, I'd look less like someone festooned for Alex, and more like the savvy businesswoman I'd always wanted to become.

"You're a genius," I said.

"You think I don't know that? Here, try it on. Bernie *sera ici dans un instant.*"

"How was that?"

"Bernie will be here in a moment. Didn't you learn French in school? Jesus. Get undressed. Come on. I've got to shovel you into a pair of Spanx. I can only hope the ice I had for dinner will give me the necessary strength to do that job."

* * *

Later, when Bernie was finished, he stepped away from me. I looked in the mirror and smiled at what I saw, and then I saw him and Blackwell standing behind me. Blackwell nodded, and I stood.

"What do you think?" I asked.

"Perfection," Bernie said. "I love it, Jennifer."

"Turn to me," Blackwell said. "That's right. Now, let me see your back. Good. Turn to the side. Now turn back to me." She brought a hand to her chest. "Well," she said. "That *is* perfect. She looks lovely. Look what we created, Bernie. Just enough of her tits are bared to capture the attention of any straight man in the group, but everything else is concealed so she can work her business magic. Or whatever it is that she does. This is the best yet. Even the gays will love it. What's most important is that this says she is serious about her work. This says she came to play ball without being threatening or emasculating."

"I *am* here in the room," I said.

"Stop being so sensitive while we admire you. And look," Blackwell said to me as she turned to a table behind her. "I didn't forget it this time. I have a small army of clutches to match every dress on that rack. Here you are. Small and black and made in the same fabric as your dress. And don't think I didn't have to hustle for that to happen, because I did. But it's all worth it. You're chic in your couture. I have to say, doing this is one of the best parts of my day when it happens. I love it."

"You're a fashionista," Bernie said to her.

"I can feel the tug of that calling—it's been there since I was a child when I eschewed that awful Sears department store my mother favored for the Bloomingdales that was just down the street."

"How did you ever cope?" asked Bernie.

"It was terrible, but I try not to analyze it. It'll only make me hate my mother more."

"You have an eye that few can match."

"It's been said before, but who am I to judge my own work?"

"A true artist would."

"Do you think?"

"I know. I've witnessed you in action. I've seen what you can do."

"*Mon dieu. C'est mon destin.*"

"Say moan what?" I asked.

"It's my destiny, Jennifer. You really need to study French. That's twice tonight that you didn't understand the simplest of words. And you're wearing Dior, for God's sake, who happens to have been French. God!"

I flashed my eyes at Bernie. "*J'aime mes cheveux,*" I said, patting my hair. "*Vous êtes un artiste. Un génie. Merci pour tout ce que vous avez fait.*"

I turned to Blackwell, whose mouth was agape. "It's nearly eight," I said lightly. "I should go. Alex will be waiting. Are we ready?"

"You're a trickster, Jennifer Kent."

"First I'm wicked. Now I'm a trickster."

"I mean it."

"*Très bien. Allons.*"

* * *

At the elevator, Blackwell gave me her usual advice before sending me off. It was something I'd grown accustomed to, and I appreciated it because she always tended to leave me with something to think about.

Once again, she didn't disappoint.

"How are you feeling?"

"Excited."

"To be with Alex? Or to do business?"

"Both. But to be honest? It's more about being thrown into the possibilities of what might happen tonight. The idea of nailing down two deals if we're lucky, is exciting to me."

"First and foremost, it's all about Henri. If you're given the chance, charm him. He loves a beautiful woman, but he loves a smart woman even more. For some unknown reason I can't fathom, you happen to be both. I think you could be the key Alex needs to get his attention. If Alex is able to get Dufort on his own, just stand there and look pretty. But if Dufort engages you, be engaging."

"Noted."

"And I don't mean only with your cleavage, Jennifer. He'll notice the twins, but what he'll really notice is your intelligence. He is nothing if not focused on taking his empire to the next level. That's what matters to him most. That's what he wants to hear. Wenn can offer that. Alex has an idea for it."

"So do I."

"Have you shared that with Alex?"

"I haven't seen Alex since we landed. So, no, I haven't."

"You might want to."

"Don't worry. If and when I offer up my own idea, I will have tested the waters first."

"You're going to be the end of me."

"But I need you."

"I know you do. It's what keeps me going, even if you did conceal from me that you obviously know French. That was just cruel of you."

"Cruel?"

"Yes, cruel. At your level, I know that one day you'll be called upon to speak French to one of Alex's international contacts, so naturally I was concerned that you'd fail. But you wouldn't, would you? You led me down a dark road of despair with your presumed lack of knowledge in the Romance languages, and then you pulled that awful surprise that you knew French all along. Terrible."

"You wouldn't have it any other way."

She studied me for a moment, and then smiled. "I suppose I wouldn't."

"Wish me well tonight?"

"Of course. And just remember, Jennifer. Be kind to him. Whatever is happening in his life right now, he's working it out on his own. Don't be slighted by such a minor detail. Enjoy your time with him. Enjoy the moments. I'm here to tell you that they don't come often. I once thought I had it all with Charles. Then... divorce. If you don't tend to the farm, it can all go wrong so quickly. But if you're good to one another, and if you respect each other's space, you can enjoy this time in your life, no matter how long it lasts, which might just be forever. Who knows?"

"I think the Romance languages have gotten the best of you, Ms. Blackwell."

She raised her eyebrows at me as the elevator doors slid open. Any trace of humor that had been there before left her face. She became stone-cold serious. "What you don't know about me, Jennifer, is that despite everything I've been through these past few months, I'm still hopeful. I'm not finished yet. It's too soon now, but I'd like to find someone else again. Even though, at my age, the cards are against me. But I'm not giving up quite yet. In fact, I'm not giving up at all. We all deserve love in our lives. Everyone uses that awful cliché that love hurts, but that's not true. Real love doesn't hurt. Real love is wonderful. It's loneliness that hurts. And rejection. And losing someone close to you hurts. Everyone confuses these things with love, but in reality, love is the only thing in this world that covers up all the pain and makes us feel wonderful again."

I stared nakedly at her, stunned by the depth of what she'd just said.

"Now, shake off whatever happened between you and Alex, and go spend some time with the man who might be the one for you."

CHAPTER EIGHTEEN

The elevator dropped to the forty-seventh floor, almost too quickly for me to collect myself. When the doors slid open, Alex was there waiting for me, just as he always was. But his hands weren't in his pockets as they usually were, and he wasn't standing so disarmingly. In fact, he looked tense to see me.

"I'm glad that you came," he said.

"It's my job."

"I hope it's more than that."

I remembered all the things that Blackwell had said to me, and I softened. I felt a deep affection for him, and I knew it was wrong to hide it. I stepped out and kissed him on the cheek. "Of course it is."

"You look lovely."

"You already know how I feel about you in a tux.

Tell me why you're so interested in Henri Dufort. I have an idea, but he's into everything. Let's see if we're on the same page."

"Why don't you begin?"

"All right. Dufort owns Streamed, which essentially is Netflix for the global market. They're expanding as rapidly as they can, but the global market is the global market, and there are dozens of closed doors. My research shows that Dufort is having difficulty breaking into some of the countries where Wenn Entertainment is already a known player. Sometimes Dufort gets lucky, but then other obstacles arise, likely because he doesn't have the relationships Wenn has with these people. In this world, relationships are everything. Dufort knows that. Wenn could partner with him in an effort to get beyond the bureaucratic bullshit. And this would make Wenn Entertainment a fortune if you struck a deal with Dufort that allowed him into the countries he wants to dominate before it's too late before other capitalize on the idea. Am I right?"

He didn't answer at once. Instead, he just stared at me.

"Well?"

"That's not what I had in mind at all."

I felt defeated. "Oh." I wasn't sure how to read him. He wasn't saying anything, but I was sure that I had disappointed him. My mind raced to the other options I'd considered before talking to him tonight. One was a good possibility, so I readied myself for it. "I'm sorry. That seemed to me to be the most logical choice. I have other ideas."

"You already have the best idea. What I had in mind was solid and potentially lucrative, but it pales next to what you're proposing. Which countries is Streamed being shut out of?"

"India. China. Brazil. Mexico. There are a host of others, some of which Netflix—Streamed's largest competitor—is just beginning to build a presence. Those markets are the largest and most coveted, and Netflix is just starting to hit them hard. But there's still time. Before it's too late and Netflix gets a stronghold, Streamed could compete if it joined forces with Wenn soon because Wenn Entertainment already has relationships in those countries, and in many other countries where Netflix isn't yet a player. I was thinking that with your contacts, you could work out a partnership with Dufort that would ease his way in. I'd imagine he'd appreciate that. I'd imagine that he'd pay handsomely for it by giving Wenn a significant stake in Streamed."

"How did you come up with this?"

I shrugged. "I spent the afternoon doing research. Dufort has much larger holdings than Streamed, but streaming video is where the money is right now, and where it's really going to be going forward. It's eventually how much of the world will view movies and television shows. It's like e-books—they're taking over because that's how most people will read one day. Same with music. When did you last buy a CD? You didn't. You downloaded it. The stats don't lie. Streamed seemed like a natural choice to me, whereas some of Dufort's other holdings were too obvious. Streamed needs and wants to grow worldwide, it has the potential to make billions. But it's having a difficult time doing so, so that's what I went with."

"You came up with a potential winner."

"What were you thinking?"

"Something the board proposed. Something more obvious. It doesn't matter now. We go with this."

"But the board is expecting something else from you."

"And I'll offer Henri both if I feel that it's the right thing to do. If I don't, I won't mention what I had in mind and will press forward with your idea. What you need to understand about the board is that as sophisticated as it is, it's not exactly on the cutting edge when it comes to emerging technologies. It's comprised of an older group of men and women who don't necessarily understand the importance of digital. They get it to a point, especially when it comes to music and maybe a bit when it comes to the importance of e-books if only because of Wenn Publishing. But they're not entirely there yet, which is understandable. Wenn Entertainment is just a small part of Wenn—it's not our most lucrative arm. The board's attention is elsewhere. As a consultant, you were brought in to give me your best advice, which you have. It's my choice as CEO to decide what happens tonight. Netflix is a force in North America, but it's relatively new to the worldwide market. Here, it's silly to challenge it. But globally? It makes sense because Netflix itself is just starting to make inroads abroad. Their brand is known here, but not so much in other markets. It's still new enough for Dufort and us to take it on and challenge it."

"I don't want to piss off the board," I said.

"Who cares if you do? You work for me. This is my decision."

"We should probably go."

"Not before I do this."

He came forward, put his hand low along my waist, and kissed me lightly on the lips. When I responded, he became more passionate. I closed my eyes and kissed him back to the point that I started to lose myself in him. He kissed me again, but then I broke away and just held him tightly, my head on his shoulder.

"I need you, Jennifer," he said in my ear.

"I owe you an apology," I said. "I'm sorry I was distant today. In Maine, suddenly there were guards everywhere. You kept talking to them during our final night together. I was so worried for you, Alex, that it made me sick. You wouldn't talk to me about it. When that happened, for whatever reason, my instinct was to pull back. I'm sorry for the way I acted."

"Don't be. There are things that happen in my life that can sound frightening, but only if you don't know how routine they are. I decided to protect you from that."

"What things?"

"It doesn't matter."

"It matters to me."

"Let's just say that what happened over the past two days happens to me often. Right now, everything is under control. I just need you to trust me if I need to handle certain events on my own. I'm not trying to keep you out. I'm trying to keep you from worrying about things that can and are being dealt with. These are things you don't need to concern yourself with."

"Will you ever fully let me in?"

"Yes, of course. One day, I'll have no choice but to tell you everything."

"When is that?"

"When I marry you," he said.

CHAPTER NINETEEN

In the limousine, we sat close to each other, my hand holding his deep in his lap and my head still spinning from what he'd said to me a moment ago. He was considering marriage? Since when? Shouldn't we date for a few months before we even got to that point?

I really need to speak to Lisa.

"Things have changed since the last time we were out together in public," I said. "Now, I'm your hired consultant, not your hired companion. How do we play this? What are we tonight? Because it'll look a bit odd if your consultant is holding your hand. I just need to know what you expect from me."

"You're my girlfriend and my consultant. As far as I'm concerned, nothing's changed. I know you're not ready for the word 'girlfriend,' and I know I probably freaked you out a moment ago with talk of marriage, but that's how I feel about you and our relationship, and I don't take those words lightly." He smiled at me. "And I'm convinced that, sooner or later, neither will you."

"You sound awfully confident."

"That's because I am. I didn't expect for this to happen to me again in my life, but it has. I'm grateful. And I'll do what it takes to make you see that I'm right."

He bent over to kiss me on the lips, then he kissed my neck, and then his head dipped lower to my breasts.

"Alex..."

"Just a kiss."

"But you can't do that to me now. I'll be a wreck if you start."

He took one of my breasts in his hands, and massaged the tip of my nipple while he gently kissed my ear. *The stubble again. It's truly going to be the end of me.*

"Please—," I begged.

"Will you join me later tonight? My place?"

"You know I will. But not here. I can't have my head in the ether, and you're driving it there now."

He reached into his inside jacket pocket and pulled out a folded piece of paper. "That's for later," he said, handing it to me. "Put it in your clutch for now. Whenever you doubt how I feel for you, read it. Steinbeck says it best. I copied a passage from his book of letters for you. All of it's in there. Everything I feel about you and about us. Read it when you're ready."

I wanted to read it right then, but he was back to nuzzling my neck. I could smell the woody scent of his cologne, and it seemed as if it was a part me of now. Sometimes, when I wasn't with him, his scent was one of the things I remembered most, and right now, it was within me.

"We're getting close," I said.

"*You're* getting close?"

I laughed. "No! Well, maybe. If you keep this up I will be. But we're almost there. Oh, that feels good. OK. Stop. I need to focus. I can't fall out of this car when we arrive, and if you don't pull it together, that's going to happen."

"You think I'm able to focus right now?" he asked. He took my hand and pressed it between his legs, where I could feel his hardness. He was teasing me, but I could tease back. *All right*, I thought. *Let's do this and see how quickly he can compose himself.* I started to stroke him in his pants, and when his head dipped back, I grabbed him in my hand, squeezing until it gave him the same kind of pleasure he gave me.

"Stop," he said.

"Why?"

"Because I get it."

"You don't want to fall out of the car?"

"I'm not sure I can leave the car like this."

"You started it."

"So I did. Can you blame me?"

"What I hope is that you can hide *that* when you get out of the car," I said, releasing him. "It's going to look like a tent."

"Same goes for your nipples."

"You're terrible." I reached for my clutch, saw the note on top of it, tucked it inside, and wondered again what it said. *Later*. I removed my compact, and turned on the light above me. "Oh, Bernie," I said. "He'd be having none of this." I patted my face with powder, and then reapplied my lipstick. I looked at Alex, who was adjusting himself in his pants.

"Tight fit?"

"You don't even know."

"Actually, I have a fairly good idea."

He grinned at me.

"We're supposed to be adults," I said, smiling.

"Oh, right. That. Well, that can go to hell if it means we can't do this."

"Do you want to neck later?"

"Very funny. And by the way, I want to do a lot more than that."

"Looks like we're here," I said as the limousine slowed and pulled left to the curb. "Are you ready for this?"

"I'm still hard."

"Good luck with that," I said.

"You're supposed to help me."

"Seriously? That thing has a mind of its own. You should be proud of it. Get out there and show the damned thing off."

"You're incorrigible."

"Look who's talking."

The driver opened the door, and flashes of lights began to pop from the crowd of reporters and paparazzi standing along the sidelines. I held out my hand to the driver and tried to step onto the sidewalk as elegantly as possible despite the length of my dress and how turned on I was. Eventually, Alex emerged from the car, and while he acknowledged the crowd with a wave, he stood close behind me for what I could only imagine was a very good reason.

"Are you able to walk?" I asked over my shoulder.

"Barely."

"Wenn's stock would skyrocket if you revealed to the world what you're packing in your pants."

"Hilarious. And by the way, it's your nipples that are going to be on Page Six tomorrow, love."

"Let them be. I earned them on the drive over here."

On impulse, I turned to him and kissed him full on the lips as our bodies were sheathed in an unimaginable display of light. Men and women called out to us. They didn't know me yet, but they absolutely knew Alex, and they egged him on to turn this way and that. To my surprise, he held me at his side. We posed for photographs, and then he returned my kiss in such a way that I knew that one or many of these photographs would go viral by morning.

And what is the board at Wenn going to think of that? I thought.

CHAPTER TWENTY

When the elevator doors opened and we arrived on the rooftop, it was teeming with people, and an orchestra was playing at the opposite end of the roof. More composed now than we were earlier, Alex took my hand in his and we walked into something that looked as if it was out of a fairytale.

How did Henri Dufort ever manage to create the gardens I saw before me now? Just getting the dirt up here alone had to have been a massive undertaking, never mind all the established bushes, flowering shrubs and grass that I saw.

At this height, the city views were magnificent. Better yet, probably because the building was buffered by the Park, which was just across the street, it wasn't as windy as I thought it would be. Instead, there was only a light breeze that was buffered by the trees he'd planted and that made the lower half of my dress seem almost weightless when the air caught the material and caused it to ripple around my ankles.

A waiter with a silver tray filled with glasses of champagne stopped beside us. Alex took a glass for each of us. We sipped and walked along the tiled surface, the lot of which was bordered by the gardens. The space was huge and carefully designed. The gardens were meant to be a spectacular feature, but not impede the deck's main purpose—entertainment.

"This is incredible," I said to Alex.

"I've seen a lot of impressive rooftops, but I have to admit, you don't see this every day."

"How did he ever manage to do this?"

"Google it. The *Times* did a big piece on it when it was finished. All the details are there. It's a good read." Something caught his eye, and he brought his glass to his lips. "Shit," he said.

"What?"

"Your old friend Tootie Staunton-Miller is here. She and her husband Addy are coming this way."

"Well, at least I like Addy."

"There's nothing not to like about him. As for her? She's a viper."

"I'm ready for her."

"You'll need to be."

"Alex!" Tootie said as she closed the distance between us. She was wearing a sleek navy blue evening dress that, even at her age, didn't betray an extra pound of body fat. She was nothing if not fit and well preserved. She gave Alex an air kiss on each cheek, and made a clear point to ignore me. "You look as handsome as ever," she said.

"Hello, Tootie. Addy," Alex said.

"Good to see you, Alex," Addy said. "And also you, Jennifer. You look more beautiful each time I see you."

"Thank you, Addy. You look pretty dapper yourself."

"I appreciate that," he said, ignoring his wife's disapproving glance. "This is a wonderful party. We arrived just after you two."

"Yes," Tootie said. "That was quite a display of affection we saw when you exited your car. All caught by the cameras. All calculated for the press."

"Excuse me?" Alex said.

"Nothing, nothing. Sorry, sorry." She shot me a glance. "It's just that's it's so unusual to see anything like that at these sorts of events. Most of us eschew the press. I nearly gasped when I saw you two entwined so romantically with each other."

"There's nothing wrong with spontaneity," Alex said. "Or romance. I rather enjoyed it. Tootie, you remember Jennifer?"

"How could I forget Jennifer? Hellohoware?"

I held up my glass of champagne. "As effervescent as ever, Tootie."

"No doubt. That's a pretty dress." She stared straight at my plunging neckline. "It's almost understated for you. Who designed it?"

"Dior."

She waved a hand in the air. "Dior, Dior. The last time I saw you, you were in Dior. You must experiment, Jennifer."

"The last time I saw you, I was in Valentino."

"Oh. I don't—"

"Remember? Care? It really doesn't matter to me. Either way, I *have* been experimenting. You should see whom I've been wearing. But you haven't. I guess we don't travel in the same circles, Tootie. I'm beginning to think that we're worlds apart. At least on some levels."

She seethed at that.

"We just returned from a brief trip to Maine," Alex said, trying his best to break the tension.

"Maine," Tootie said. "That's right. That's where you're from, isn't it, Jennifer? Inland, I believe?"

"That's right, Tootie. Inland."

"I can see why you got out. Manhattan offers so much more."

"Manhattan has its perks. But Maine? I love Maine."

"Really? Even inland?"

"Even inland. The people are real there. Nobody is fake or pretends to be something that they aren't. You can go anywhere and feel welcomed there, not judged. Never judged. I love inland Maine for that very reason. In fact, I count on it for that."

"How interesting."

"Is it interesting?"

"I find it interesting."

"Then that's what's interesting. As for the coast of Maine, which you'd probably enjoy, it's another story all together. The Rockefellers have several estates there. And then there are the Morgans and the Vanderbilts. And obviously the Astors and the Fords, who have estates that would leave even you breathless, Tootie. Or maybe they wouldn't—who knows what impresses you? Also, a fair amount of Hollywood lives there, though I doubt if you care a trace about them because none of them are in the book. Still, you get the idea. Maine calls people to its coast. It's special. And really, if you don't want to be disappointed in Maine, as I sense you might be if you somehow found yourself stranded inland for instance, you just need to know where to go. For instance, the ocean isn't so far from where I used to live. In Bar Harbor, there's a fantastic place called Thunder Hole. You should see it, Tootie."

"It sounds to me like some awful theme park ride for children."

"It's actually an impressive display of nature. When the tide surges in, it offers up an angry, almost violent explosion of water that tunnels into the sky. I think you'd take to it quite readily."

"I don't know what that means."

"It's not important."

"Did Alex meet your family while you were there? I'd love to hear about *that*."

"We went down to the Point," Alex said. "You remember our home there, Tootie. You went with Mother several times. Probably Twenty years ago. Jennifer and I decided to visit, and to take some time out for ourselves."

"That sounds romantic," Addy said, clearly annoyed with his wife.

"It was, Addy."

"I can only imagine how romantic it was," Tootie replied.

I'd probably hear about it later, but I didn't care. I leaned toward her, and said, "You have no idea. I'm still sore."

Her mouth fell open, and I saw Addy try to suppress a smile. Alex took a long pull on his champagne and reached for my free hand.

"It was good to see you, Addy," I said.

Addy's eyes twinkled. "It's always good to see *you*, Jennifer."

"And you, Tootie. Seeing you always is a curiosity of insights."

"What does that mean?"

I decided to let her figure it out on her own. Alex and I started to walk forward into the crowd. "Enjoy your evening," I said.

CHAPTER TWENTY-ONE

"Thunder Hole?" Alex said in a bemused voice as we walked into the crowd. "Really?"

"I'd like shove her into it. She obviously doesn't like me."

"I'd say it's mutual."

"If she had been civil toward me the first time we met, I never would have behaved that way. But she wasn't—she was a snob. She looked down upon me. Remember? I'm not in the book. Oh, how she brings out the devil in me. I hope I didn't embarrass you."

He squeezed my hand. "Actually, I wanted to laugh a few times. So did Addy—I could see it on his face. She's a nasty woman—always has been. That's probably one of the reasons she and my mother were such good friends. Nasty attracts nasty. I've never liked her, either." He leaned toward my ear. "Are you really still sore?"

"Not *that* sore."

"Good to hear."

"Naughty boy. So, where is Dufort?"

"Holding court over there. Do you see? Down about halfway to your right. It looks as if he's sitting in some kind of antique gilt chair."

"It's like a throne. And why not? He's king here tonight. How old is he today, anyway?"

"The invitation said he was celebrating his sixtieth, but everyone here knows it's at least his seventieth. Though I have to hand it to him—he looks good for his age."

"He probably pays his toxes."

"He pays his what?"

"Botox. His toxes."

"You're in a mood tonight," he said. "I like you like this. It means you're going to be fun in bed later."

"You really need to focus, Alex. That's me consulting you. That's me earning my salary right there."

"Noted."

I stopped walking and became serious. "Look who else is here."

"Who?"

"About a hundred feet ahead of us. Just to your left. Darius Stavros and his son, Cyrus. We probably should go over and say hello to them."

"I'd prefer that Cyrus gets nowhere near you."

"We're beyond that now, aren't we?"

"I suppose we are."

"You don't have to worry about me with Cyrus or with anyone else."

"Why's that?"

"Because I'm with you."

He clutched my hand harder. "You don't say that enough for me. You don't know what that means to me. I'm trying my best to convince you to come closer to me, but you keep throwing up walls."

"I didn't this weekend."

"I don't mean physical. I mean mental. Emotional."

"Alex, you're the only man I've ever been interested in. You're the only man I've *been* with. Doesn't that tell you something?"

"It does."

"It should tell you everything you need to know about where I stand in this relationship. Let's just enjoy what we have. Let me work through my trust issues. The more I'm with you and the more seamlessly things go between us, the more those walls of mine will come down. But right now? Now, we're here, and I'm happy to be here. I'm eager for what's coming later, after the party, when it's just the two of us. But we're working now. As your consultant—and I'm not joking about this—we need to go over and do our duty. Through Cyrus, you got your deal with Stavros Shipping. We have to go over and greet each of them in order to keep everyone happy so that when it comes time to renew the contract, we're able to just slide into it without a hitch."

"You're right," he said. "Let's do it."

In my clutch, I felt my cell buzz, which likely was a text from Lisa. "Just two seconds," I said. "She knows I'm here, and would never interrupt unless it was important. Let me check." I put my glass of champagne down on the table next to me.

"Take your time. I'm in no hurry to see Cyrus."

"Cyrus is greasy, but he got you the deal," I sang as I removed my cell.

"So he did."

I flicked on my phone and saw that it wasn't a text, but an email sent to the corporate account I had with Wenn. Its subject line read, "Dead soon. Maybe tonight. Maybe tomorrow. Or not. But soon." I didn't recognize the sender's address, and was about to delete it as SPAM when I noticed that there was an attachment. Out of curiosity, I clicked on it, and a photo of me leaving the limousine when we first arrived here tonight filled the screen. I felt a chill.

"Is she OK?" Alex asked.

"It's not from Lisa."

"Who's it from?"

"I don't know."

He turned to me. "You sound tense. Is something wrong?"

I needed time to process this, and didn't want to send him off his game before he spoke to Dufort. I deflected. "Let's say hello to Darius and Cyrus, then you can work your magic with Dufort. Then we can go back to your place."

"What did you just receive?"

As unnerved as I was, I still wasn't sharing this with him now, so I kept focused on the task at hand. "I'll tell you later, but time is running out. We have work to do. You're getting that deal with Dufort. Or at least you're going to tempt him with it. Come on," I said, putting my phone in my clutch and willing myself to relax. I was shaken, but I couldn't let it show here. I smiled at him. "Let's finish this so we can go home and tend to some unfinished business."

* * *

Thirty minutes later, our conversation with Darius and Cyrus over, Alex spoke with Dufort while I hung back and watched the crowd.

I recognized many of the guests from their photographs in the *Times*, in the *Journal*, on television or on the Internet, but I also recognized two other faces in the crowd, one of whom was looking at me with open hostility.

It was Immaculata Almendarez. Alex had snubbed her at the fundraiser for the National Museum of Art when she had tried to set Alex and me up by having us sit next to her at dinner so she could belittle me by flirting with Alex. All of that failed spectacularly for her when Alex took her down with a fistful of words before he got us another table. Here, she was with an older gentleman who looked familiar to me. And then I recognized him—Richard Gould, the CEO of AT&T.

I glanced away from her and looked over at Gordon Kobus, whose airline Alex was preparing to take over. He was talking to a beautiful blonde woman half his age, thus underscoring the playboy reputation Alex had told me he was known for.

I watched him for a moment, and was surprised when he turned his attention to me. His face showed no sense of surprise at seeing me here, which suggested that he'd already seen Alex and me. Instead, he just held my gaze while his mouth tightened into a thin line of hatred. I'd done nothing to the man, but apparently my association with Alex was enough for Kobus to take a dislike of me, especially because he knew that Alex was currently wooing Kobus' management team in an effort to make the potential takeover go smoothly.

Did one of them send me that email? Or did it come from someone else on this roof? I wondered if I was being paranoid. Certainly, the people in this room had better things to do than send threats.

Or did they? Over the years, since he'd assumed control of Wenn, Alex had made his share of enemies. He'd undertaken several hostile takeovers, and by merging his company with others in an effort to downsize, he'd left plenty without work in an already difficult economy.

As friendly as everyone appeared to be tonight— with the exceptions of Immaculata and Kobus—I could sense a toxic undercurrent, likely because I still was an outsider and not used to playing their games. Dufort had invited the most powerful men and women in the city to his birthday bash, all of whom were competitive overachievers who knew that at any moment, any person on this roof could turn against them in ways that might ruin them.

Perhaps now more than ever, I saw Alex's professional life as it was, and I didn't like any of it. At least not the social part of it. Working behind the scenes as his consultant was another story. That made perfect sense to me because I knew I could benefit him there. But this was now the third time I'd played dress up and gone out to a party with him, only to have a snob, a competitor, or a woman who wanted Alex for herself look down upon me. I'd never played those kinds of games with anyone, but without question, that sort of behavior was deeply rooted here.

I looked over at Alex, and saw, with a sense of relief, that he had Dufort's attention—the man was listening intently to him and was often nodding as Alex spoke. All good signs. I hoped he was teasing Dufort just enough to get a meeting with the man.

A server stopped beside me and asked if I'd like a canapé, but I declined. I looked around the space with a sense of cynicism I didn't have when we first arrived—and for good reason. Since then, I'd had to deal with the email, and then the harsh looks from Immaculata and Kobus.

I thought about the email, and was convinced that it either came from somebody who was here right now, or from somebody who obviously wanted to rattle Alex by using me as a target. Whoever sent it was expecting me to share it with him for that reason, but should I? Was someone seriously out to kill me? Now that I'd had time to reflect, the idea seemed absurd to me. What initially felt like a genuine threat, now felt more like a cheap prank that I shouldn't be concerned with.

Whoever sent it didn't exactly have to be a genius. I was on Wenn's website. My email address was listed there. If, for whatever reason, someone wanted to shake Alex by threatening me, they had everything they needed—my email address, a photo taken of me when we arrived tonight, and a death threat. All were effective. As Alex continued to talk to Dufort, I decided to enjoy the rest of the night and dismiss the email as a jolt intended to throw me—and potentially him—off guard.

Welcome to the world of big business, I thought. *Maybe this is what Alex was talking about yesterday when he said that whatever was happening to him was normal and under control. Maybe this is my new normal. Maybe I need to accept that.*

I thought of the note Alex gave me. While he was with Dufort, I finally saw my chance to read it. I turned my back to him, and removed it from my clutch. I unfolded it and was surprised by how long it was. It wasn't a note, but a letter. With a sense of trepidation, I read it.

At the top of the page, in his own handwriting, he wrote, "This is from *Steinbeck: A Life in Letters*. It's one of my favorite books. When we were in Maine, whenever I saw you or thought of you, I thought of this, because I'm in love with you, Jennifer. Steinbeck wrote this letter to a friend of his. It reminded me again of how short life is, not that I need to be reminded after what happened to Diana. But still. I wanted you to know how I feel about you. I know now that life is too short to not tell you. For me, there's no shame in telling you exactly how I feel about you—and about us—even if you feel differently."

I brought a finger to my mouth and closed my eyes. No man had ever said that he was in love with me. And for him to say so in a letter was intentional— it meant that I could always revisit this moment. He didn't want it to be something I would remember in a blur—he wanted it to be something tangible that I could return to whenever I wanted to. I couldn't process my own thoughts or feelings at that point— they were scattered. Overwhelmed. Instead, I just started to read.

"There are several kinds of love," Steinbeck's passage began. "One is a selfish, mean, grasping, egotistical thing which uses love for self-importance. This is the ugly and crippling kind. The other is an outpouring of everything good in you—of kindness and consideration and respect—not only the social respect of manners but the greater respect which is recognition of another person as unique and valuable. The first kind can make you sick and small and weak but the second can release in you strength, and courage and goodness and even wisdom you didn't know you had.

"You say this is not puppy love. If you feel so deeply—of course it isn't puppy love.

"But I don't think you were asking me what you feel. You know better than anyone. What you wanted me to help you with is what to do about it—and that I can tell you.

"Glory in it for one thing and be very glad and grateful for it.

"The object of love is the best and most beautiful. Try to live up to it.

"If you love someone—there is no possible harm in saying so—only you must remember that some people are very shy and sometimes the saying must take that shyness into consideration.

"Girls have a way of knowing or feeling what you feel, but they usually like to hear it also.

"It sometimes happens that what you feel is not returned for one reason or another—but that does not make your feeling less valuable and good."

He ended the note with this: "For me, it's the second kind of love that I feel for you. I'm saying this to you now not because I don't want to say it in person—I plan to do so soon—but so that you have a love letter from me. People don't write love letters anymore, but I think they're important. I think letters between lovers are romantic. It can define a relationship. Lift it. I wanted you to know in writing how much you mean to me. In time, I hope you feel the same as I do. I'm looking forward to that day. I do love you, Jennifer. Now, you know that. I love you—Alex."

With a dizzying sensation, I carefully folded the note and put it in my clutch. I took a breath and looked out at the city, which seemed to sigh back at me with a breeze that encompassed me. My pulse raced. At that moment, my father's voice started to encroach and steal away my happiness, but I pushed him away with a strength I'd never possessed. I denied him access to this moment, I shut him out of this moment, and I locked the door so he couldn't find a way inside. I was determined to savor this letter without interruption from the corrupt, abusive drunk who happened to be my father.

Did I love Alex? I wasn't sure. What was love? It was a foreign concept to me, at least romantic love was. Steinbeck didn't address sex when he spoke above love. Instead, he went to the core of what love was, saying the best kind of love gave you strength, courage, goodness and even wisdom you didn't know you had. That's what being with Alex was like for me.

Am I in love with him?

Before I could answer the question, Alex came up beside me and put his arm around my waist. His sudden presence gave me a start, but I stilled it. "You jumped me," I said.

"Sorry." I turned to him, and he looked happy. He kissed me gently on the cheek and asked if I was ready to go.

"Let's stay for a bit."

"But you said that you wanted to leave?"

"I've changed my mind. People are dancing near the orchestra. How about a dance, and then we can leave?"

"I'd love that. I'd love to dance with you again."

Am I in love with you?

"First, how did it go with Dufort?"

"He's intrigued. He knows that Wenn Entertainment is in the countries he can't seem to get into. We're going to meet on Friday. I think we'll come to some sort of collaboration."

"That's fantastic."

"You're the one who thought of it."

"You're the one who sold it to him."

"Which makes us one hell of a team."

"It does."

And it did. In so many ways.

"Later, I want you tell me about the idea you had in mind for him," I said. "At that meeting, you might want to pitch it to him. Because of your contacts, a lot of goodwill will be between you at that point. That's an opportunity for more business."

He dropped his voice and pressed his mouth against my ear. "You know what opportunity I want? I want to be with you now."

"Well, there's a change in subject."

"I'm serious."

"Probably best not to do so here. Immaculata is here tonight, and she's been tossing me daggers since you've been with Dufort."

"Immaculata is here?"

"Mmm-hmm. She's with Richard Gould."

"The AT&T Richard Gould?"

"That's right."

"So, that's how she got in. Fine. Let her lose herself in him. I'm all for it. Let's dance. And then let's get out of here. I want to get you into bed. There are all kind of things I want to do to you. And to say to you. In fact, you're not going to know what hit you when I'm finished."

Funny, because I already didn't know what had hit me.

CHAPTER TWENTY-TWO

When we left the party after an intimate waltz, during which Immaculata made it a point to step away from her date and openly watch us, Alex texted his driver on the elevator ride down, and then he pressed me against one of the walls. It was a long drop to the lobby, and he used every second of it to run his hands along my body before he knelt before me, lifted my dress, and kissed my sex.

"In about fifteen minutes, I'm going to lick you here," he said, kissing me on the spot where he was going to lick me. "And here. And maybe here where you're already wet. In fact, I will go there. And my tongue is definitely going in there." He looked up at me. "But why wait fifteen minutes when I can have you now?"

In a flash, he turned around and pressed a button that stopped the elevator. Likely knowing he didn't have much time before an alarm sounded, he fell back on his knees, lifted my dress, pulled down my panties, and covered me with his mouth. His tongue pressed against my folds and swirled around them for a moment before he entered me with his tongue. I gasped at the sensation and instinctively reached out a hand, put it on the back of his head, and pulled him closer to me.

As risky as this was, none of it felt wrong. I looked above us for a camera tucked within one of the corners, but I didn't see any. Not that I cared much. I was with Alex Wenn. What was anyone going to say or do to us for what he was doing to me now?

I ran my hand through his hair, and whimpered as he brought me closer to the edge. I could feel his breath hot against my thighs while he eagerly and successfully tried to please me. I thought about the letter he wrote to me and how he said that he was in love with me. And despite confusing this moment for me because I didn't know what to make of it, or even how to process it, the way he laid himself bare to me in that letter actually fueled me now.

For the first time in my life, I felt whole. I ground myself into him and came almost at once. I cried out, but he didn't stop. He went deeper. When he was satisfied, he pulled out and flicked his tongue over my clit. Then he brushed across it with the stubble on his chin, which made me come again, this time to the point that my knees buckled.

And then the alarm went off.

Quickly, Alex slid out from under my dress and hit a button. The alarm stopped and the elevator lurched into motion again. He took a handkerchief out of his pocket and wiped his mouth while looking at me with an arched eyebrow before he came over and kissed me hard on my lips.

"Those are your first two for tonight," he said.

I was practically panting. I pulled up my panties as the elevator slowed, and shot him a look as I tried to steady myself. "That was incredible."

"That was just the beginning."

The elevator stopped, and Alex shot me a sexy, mischievous look. The doors slid open, and I reached for his hand, which I leaned into because my body was still weak from what he'd just done to me.

We walked across the lobby, went through a door that was held open for us, and slipped into the night. Ahead of us was the car. It wasn't the limousine we usually took—this time it was a large, beautiful black Mercedes. It looked different from any other

Mercedes I'd ever seen—it looked like a tank. A brute of a man was standing beside the rear door and holding it open for us. Just looking at him, I knew he was one of Alex's guards, but I said nothing. Another man was at the wheel. I glanced around and took in Manhattan at night. Light reflected off glass. Traffic roared down Fifth. On the sidewalk, pedestrians either strolled or walked at a quick clip.

We were nearly at the car when gunshots rang out.

"Rifle!" the man holding the door said.

People on the sidewalk screamed.

Everything else that happened in that moment was a blur.

I was propelled into the car so hard that my head struck the door as I slid across the seat.

Another gunshot sounded, ripping into the sky.

Behind me, I heard another scream. It was a woman. I heard people run. I heard people shout. Chaos had found its place here, and it rooted itself in an effort to bloom.

The driver got out of the car, pulled out a gun, and hurried over to Alex. I heard him order Alex into the car, but Alex was shouting something to the man who held the door open for us. I saw the man break into a run and rush down the sidewalk. Then I saw the driver get behind Alex and shove him toward the open door.

Another gunshot fired, but this time something went terribly wrong. Something connected with Alex's chest. Winded, he collapsed onto me just as the door slammed shut behind him.

The driver got back into the front seat, swung around, and reached out a hand to grab Alex's arm.

"Were you hit?"

It was difficult for him to breathe. Frightened, I put my hands on his body. I felt for the warmth of blood, but he was at the wrong angle. I cupped his face, and saw that he was struggling to breathe. Somewhere, he was hit. I was sure of it.

"Stay with me!" I shouted. "Don't you dare leave me!"

The driver was trying to assess Alex, but he should have been driving. Getting us to a hospital. I glared at him.

"He's hurt," I said. "Shot! Do something, for Christ's sake!"

The car sped away.

CHAPTER TWENTY-THREE

"Were you shot?" I asked Alex as we raced through the streets toward whatever hospital the driver was taking us to.

He lifted his head, blinked, and finally was able to catch his breath. He turned over on the seat, and pressed his hand against his chest, but I could see that his shirt was dry, not wet with blood. I felt to make sure. He was dry.

"No," he said. "When I was pushed inside, I think my chest connected with the edge of the door. It knocked the wind out of me and I fell on top of you." He struggled to sit up and I put my hand on his knee. "I'm OK," he said.

"Are you sure?"

"I'm sure."

I turned to the driver, whom I also knew was one of Alex's guards since he carried a gun. I laced into him. "What the hell was that?" I said.

"A scare tactic. They were using a rifle. If they wanted to shoot him, they would have."

"Who are *they*?"

"We don't know yet."

"Where were they shooting from?"

"If I had to guess, I'd say from one of the buildings across the street."

"So they knew we were here tonight."

"Apparently."

"What's this about?"

"We don't know."

"When are you going to know? How long has this been going on?"

"For a while," Alex said. He hesitated before he spoke, but then he seemed to make a decision, and turned to me. "For the past week, I've been receiving death threats."

"Death threats?"

"Another one came in this morning."

"Came in how?"

"On my cell. A text."

"What did it say?"

"I don't want to worry you with that."

"You think I'm not worried after what just happened? After being shot at? And after that admission? Of course I'm worried. What did it say?"

"That I'll be dead soon."

He saw the look of fear that crossed my face, and stopped me before I could say anything. "Security is looking into it. If we need to bring in the FBI, we will."

"Who would want to kill you?"

"Take your pick. Wenn has taken over dozens of companies and corporations. We've driven people out of business. People have lost their jobs because of us. My father was a frequent target of threats. As I said, this is nothing new for me, with the exception of what just happened. No threat has ever risen to that level. Otherwise, I'm used to it."

"What kind of life is that?"

"The life I inherited from my father."

My heart started to pound in my ears. I thought I'd nearly lost him, which at this point in our relationship was incomprehensible to me. I was frightened to my core. I couldn't lose him now. "This started when we were in Maine, didn't it?"

"It started before we went to Maine."

I couldn't help feeling a spark of anger and betrayal. "And you didn't tell me before we left? You knew about this, and still we had sex? Why would you do that to me? I'm emotionally invested in you now."

"Do you believe for a minute that I'm not as emotionally invested in you? Perhaps even more than you are in me? When we were in Maine, I still thought this was just another one of those pranks. Another fake threat. I've had dozens of them. And I didn't initiate what happened between us that first night in Maine, Jennifer. You did."

"You still could have have stopped it. You knew how vulnerable I was at that point. You knew what I was giving up. Why didn't you stop it, especially with this threat against your life? You should have stopped it. With the knowledge you had, nothing should have happened that night, or on the beach, or in the elevator a moment ago. I'm intimate with you now in ways that I shouldn't be."

He didn't answer.

"What did you think was going to happen when we went to Maine?"

"I didn't know."

"Oh, please. We both knew."

I collected myself and focused on the real matter at hand—his safety, my safety and how we could end this now so we could move forward with our lives. "When will you get the FBI involved?"

"Probably tomorrow."

"Why tomorrow? Why not just bring them in now? This is serious."   And then I knew why. "Because of the press, right? You're worried about how news of this might affect Wenn's stock."

"That's right. So is the board."

"Screw the board. Screw Wenn. Your safety comes first. Certainly the FBI can keep this quiet. They're the FBI for God's sake. Get your team on the phone and get the investigation started. You said you've been receiving texts. Texts are sent through cell phones. Certainly, a name is attached to that cell phone."

"You're being naïve."

"How am I being naïve?"

"There are text services, Jennifer. Some of them offer a free trial—with no credit card attached. All they require is an email address, which both of us know can be bogus. And then there are TracFone's. Do you know what *they* are? You pick them up at places like Wal-Mart, Best Buy, Target. Wherever. They come pre-loaded with minutes. Nothing is traceable to the person who holds the phone, especially if that person paid for it in cash. It offers complete anonymity until you add more minutes via a credit card. If a TracFone is what this person used to send me those texts, don't you think they'd just get another one when their minutes ran out rather than expose their identities to the world? Of course they would. You're not seeing all sides of this. Those are just two right off the top of my head. I'm sure the FBI knows of a slew of other ways to send an anonymous text. And by the way—the number attached to the texts I was sent? When you call it, you get nothing. They're not picking up for obvious reasons. I've tried."

"I don't believe for a minute that the FBI doesn't have the necessary skills and tools to deal with this kind of situation. What's getting in your way now is you and your goddamned company. You hired me as a consultant—"

"—a *business* consultant."

"That's right, and that's the advice I'm going to offer you now. Get the FBI on this. Let them do their work. Let them make this go away. If and when news hits that there was a threat against your life, we'll be prepared to tell the press that we're dealing with it. We'll do our homework beforehand. We'll counter with a shitload of news about other CEOs who have been similarly targeted, and make it sound as commonplace as it is. Just read the *Times* or the *Journal*. Or pay attention to the news in general. Or maybe even listen to a bit of common sense. Any person of great power—and that would be you, Alex—is vulnerable at any point in their lives. Your investors know that. They'd be fools not to. I don't see how any of this could affect Wenn. Spin it correctly, and it might even be a win for Wenn."

"And how do you figure that?"

"There's no such thing as bad press, Alex. If there's a way to spin this, should we need to, I'll find it."

"And you have the skills to do that?"

The comment offended me. In fact, the entire conversation offended me. "I have the skills to look the CEO of a major corporation in the eye, and set him straight in ways that no one else dares to. Bite on that for a while, because you and I know that everything I just said to you is on point. Call your surveillance team and tell them to contact the FBI."

"Take us home," Alex said to the driver. "I don't need to see a doctor." He looked at me, and on his face was an apology. "I didn't know it would go this far. I've been threatened with my life many times since I was handed Wenn, and each time, it was a prank. Obviously, this isn't. I thought I could shield you from it, but clearly that's not the case."

"It isn't," I said.

He looked at me.

"Here's something else you need to know," I said. "Tonight, *I* received a death threat. I also thought it was a prank, or I would have told you the moment it happened, especially if I'd known about this. If I'd know about this, I would have told you immediately."

He looked horrified. "What did it say?"

"That I'd be dead soon. It included an attached photograph of me, which was taken tonight. Whoever sent it to me was in the crowd when we exited the limousine. In the photo, I'm wearing this dress. They were within a few feet of me, and they threatened me with my life. How on Earth could you not have told me about this earlier? You've put your life in jeopardy, and mine as well."

"I should have taken it seriously. I'm sorry. It's just so routine—"

"I don't care if it was routine in the past. At this point, routine just ended. Now, *I'm* involved. Those bullets that were fired could have been meant for me, not you. Have you considered that? The public knows we're a couple and they know that you lost Diana. Someone could want to take me away from you, too. For whatever reason, someone might want to kill me to send either a direct threat or message to you."

He just stared at me at a loss for words.

"You should have told me about all of this when it first started," I said. "I knew something was going on. I asked you about it while we were in Maine, but you refused to tell me. And by not telling me so I could be prepared for this, you've put my life at risk."

"I didn't think it would go this far."

"Well, it has. And I don't need to hear anymore. I've heard enough. I've got it." I leaned toward the driver. "I want to get out."

"That's not a good idea, Ms. Kent."

"Pull over and let me out. I'm taking a cab from here. Do it now, or I'll open the door and jump out."

He pulled to the left and stopped the car. I grabbed my clutch, got out of the car, and started down the sidewalk.

Alex came after me.

"Get back in the car where it's safe," he said.

"Where it's safe? Seriously, Alex? Right now, nowhere is safe."

"That's a bulletproof car. Get back inside."

In my clutch, my cell buzzed, which sent a jolt of terror through me.

It could be Lisa, I thought. But I knew better.

Behind me, I could hear Alex coming closer. Right now, I didn't want him anywhere near me, so I kept moving as I removed my phone and saw that it wasn't a text. It was another email. I selected it, and my heart went cold as I stopped to read the words on the screen.

"What is it?" Alex said.

I read it again.

"What does it say?"

I turned the screen around so he could read it himself.

"You're going to die with him," the email said. "Sooner than later, you'll both be dead. Say your goodbyes now, Jennifer. Give him that last kiss on the sidewalk. You know, while you still have the chance. We'll give you two a moment to do so before we blow you apart."

This story unfolds over the course of multiple novels—not novellas. Each one follows the continuing story of Jennifer Kent and Alexander Wenn. Each book is a full-length novel with substance, not a few chapters meant to tease you along.

Continue the *Annihilate Me* series when Volume Three hits on September 20, 2013. At a discounted price, you also can pre-order it here: http://amzn.to/11k7rPB. The price will increase after the pre-order period. Depending on reader response, there might be a next book in the series.

Please join my mailing list here so you never miss a new book: http://on.fb.me/16T4y1u

Also, join me on Facebook: http://on.fb.me/ZSr29Z. I love to chat with my readers. There, I also do giveaways. I'll see you there soon!

If you would leave a review of this book on Amazon, I'd appreciate it. Reviews are critical to every writer. Thank you!

CPSIA information can be obtained at www.ICGtesting.com
Printed in the USA
LVOW01s1136271013

358775LV00001B/26/P